WILD HARBOUR

Ian Macpherson (1905–44), was born in Forres and educated at Newtonmore, Laurencekirk and Mackie Academy, Stonehaven. He graduated from Aberdeen University in 1928 with a first class honours degree in English. He spent the next two years writing his first novel *Shepherds' Calendar* which was published in 1931. This book, which has been compared to Grassic Gibbon's *Sunset Song*, draws on his own rural background to tell of a young man's growth to maturity in a farming community dominated by hard toil and the influence of the seasons.

Macpherson continued to live in his native north east, working at farming, broadcasting and writing. In the next five years he produced three further novels, including *Land of Our Fathers* (1933), and *Pride in the Valley* (1936), which are set in Speyside. His last book, *Wild Harbour* (1936), is also set in the Highlands, but it tells of the world destroyed by a future war, forebodings of which were already discernible in Europe.

Ian Macpherson died in a motorcycle accident in 1944.

Ian Macpherson

WILD HARBOUR

Introduced by John Burns

CANONGATE
CLASSICS
27

First published in Great Britain in 1936 by Methuen
and Co. Ltd. First published as a Canongate Classic in
1989 by Canongate Publishing Limited, 17 Jeffrey
Street, Edinburgh EHI IDR. Copyright © Estate of
Ian Macpherson. Introduction copyright © John
Burns 1989.

The publishers gratefully acknowledge general sub-
sidy from the Scottish Arts Council towards the
Canongate Classics series and a specific grant towards
this volume.

Set in 10pt Plantin by Hewertext Composition
Services, Edinburgh. Printed and bound in Great
Britain by Cox and Wyman, Reading.

Canongate Classics
Series Editor: Roderick Watson
Editorial Board: Tom Crawford, J. B. Pick

British Library Cataloguing in Publication Data
Macpherson, Ian, 1905–44
Wild harbour. – (Canongate classics)
I. Title
823'.912 [F]

ISBN 0-86241-234-X

Introduction

You will read very few other books like Ian Macpherson's *Wild Harbour*. It is one of those rare books that truly haunts the mind long after it has been put back on the shelf. It is a uniquely personal response to the doubts and uncertainties which many people felt in the 1930s with the darkness of war looming ever nearer, but it is written with such intensity of vision and the narrative builds with such a cumulative urgency that the reader is still keenly aware of its relevance fifty years later.

Published in 1936 it tells of the outbreak of the Second World War, a war which did not actually begin until three years later, although Macpherson has it break out in 1944. This is just part of the book's fascination; the urge to discover just how far the prophetic novelist 'got it right'. Looking back with the advantage of hindsight there are clearly areas where he got it wrong, but as Donald Campbell has pointed out this does not really matter: the detail may be wrong, but the general feeling of hopelessness and horror at the spread of war is genuine and is powerfully present throughout. As Campbell points out, 'there were many places in continental Europe . . . which must have borne a very close resemblance to the landscape of *Wild Harbour* in the summer of 1944'.[1]

Macpherson's real focus, though, is not on the war as such, but on the relationship of a man and his wife who decide to have nothing to do with the fighting and who seek refuge in the hills to avoid being drawn into the violence. Hugh and Terry set up home in a cave they had discovered some years earlier in the area around Loch Ericht and Ben Alder, a deserted and desolate area right in the heart of Scotland. The book, written as a journal, describes the way in which Hugh and Terry plan and effect their escape from the destructive horror of the modern world: and in the urgency of its ending shows how that world catches up with them.

Living under the threat of war, 'a prey to whispers, racked by fears', Hugh and Terry had often discussed what they would do if it did actually happen and the subject provided material for at least one lengthy debate with their stalker friend Duncan as to whether modern man could survive in the wilds, or whether he has 'gone soft'. For Duncan there seems little doubt that civilisation has weakened man in body and in spirit to such an extent that survival in the wilderness would no longer be a viable option.

> 'If we were forced to live by our own efforts, how'd we thrive? It stands to reason we couldn't do it. Our senses are blunted. We depend on a multitude of people to make our clothes and food and tools for us. We have noses that can't smell, ears that are deaf . . .'

Hugh, on the other hand, sees man's intelligence as the factor which would enable him to survive and feels sure that if driven to it man would find within himself qualities and potentialities he has long since forgotten. In taking himself and his wife into the wilderness he *has* to discover these qualities to keep them alive. Intelligence, he quickly realises, is not just the theorising intellect. It is not that kind of intelligence that sustains them so long, but a combination of mental *and* physical agility and resilience.

Macpherson himself makes no attempt in the book to argue a case for pacifism. He is much more concerned to involve his reader imaginatively in the plight of his two central characters through the device of the journal, and to highlight the futility of war by showing how valuable are the things it destroys. In the face of a war which threatens to engulf the world, Hugh and Terry desperately try to preserve their love for each other, and on that level their story must be emblematic of all those other human bonds and relationships broken apart by wars since the beginning of time. The reader is constantly made aware of their vulnerability. At times they are described clinging to each other like children lost in a threatening world they do not understand. At times they are seen as anxious, frightened figures against a background of disturbing apocalyptic imagery: 'the future had no light; we

lived on the edge of a world gone mad'. As their isolation
from the rest of the world deepens and their nerves begin to
crack under the strain of it all they begin to argue with each
other. Whatever their faults, perhaps because of their faults,
the reader is moved to care about these characters because in
them is revealed much of our own human frailty and vulnerability.

We respond, too, to the desire to find a secret place where
we can be safe from the pressures of the outside world which
even in peacetime can sometimes threaten to overwhelm us.
On a simple level the game of building a den where we can
feel secure and in control is something we have all done as
children. For Hugh and Terry it is no game: it is quite simply
a matter of life or death.

Initially things go reasonably well for them and there is a
great sense of achievement in making their escape and
starting to build a home for themselves: domesticating part
of the wilderness which sustains them. Gradually their new
life begins to seem more real than the life they had left
behind, which now seems 'trivial', and the otherwise desolate
country becomes for them a place of sanctuary; a 'sanctuary
of the mind' as Hugh puts it at one point. The hard work
takes their minds off the fears and anxieties which lie always
at the back of their minds.

> [Terry] began to laugh like a happy child and dance
> amongst the peats, waving her bare peat-smeared arms
> over her head.

> We bathed in Loch Coulter; we lay at the mouth of
> our cave to attend night's summer shade; we saw the
> rough hills climb up against the sky and it grew dark
> enough for stars to shine. There are moments when
> misery departs that require no voice; we waited in
> silence until night reached its deepest, though it was
> only the twilight still.

Despite passages like this which celebrate a new-found
awareness of the beauty and mystery of life, the guilt and
anxiety caused by feeling they are safe at the expense of
others lies just below the surface. It comes out in the care
with which they try to keep their cave camouflaged against
prying eyes by making sure that the stones used to block one

entrance have their weathered side outward. It comes out, too, in the way Hugh stalks different areas for game so as not to frighten away the wildlife from their immediate vicinity. It is also there in the way Hugh and Terry constantly monitor the weather and the changing seasons. As the journal goes on it becomes clear that the approach of winter is a powerful metaphor for the end; the coldness and darkness of death.

Perhaps most tellingly their anxieties have a destructive effect on their feelings for each other, so that the relationship they are so desperate to protect becomes strained almost to breaking point. Hugh in particular seems unable to live up to his early idealism, and often treats Terry with a 'defensive roughness' that he cannot control, though it is obviously hurtful to her. In a sense this was bound to happen for all along Hugh has had doubts about their position. Time and again Terry has had to coax him out of depression or out of rages about the hopelessness of it all. All along Terry has had a simple but unshakeable faith that they are doing the right thing.

Finally anxiety forces itself upon them in the shape of desperate bands of armed men who break into the closed world around their cave. From this point on their isolation is ended and the anxiety is no longer just in their minds: it is stalking them just as surely as Hugh had earlier stalked the deer. This time there can be no escape: they must face it. Again it is Terry who does so most fully, even though she knows it is the beginning of the end for them. As they are drawn in to the fighting they respond differently. Hugh finds a 'fierce exultation' in it, while Terry finds comfort in helping one of the wounded men even though he dies.

Having lived for so long on the edges of the human world this renewed involvement releases them both from the inner anxieties that had begun to destroy them. They decide to leave the cave and go back to the world of men, whatever might await them, a decision which liberates them from doubt and fear because once more they feel in control of their own lives. This does not negate their experience because it is only through living as they have done that they have been able to break through to this new sense of being, the unselfish acceptance of a responsibility to others, an acknowledgement that however misguided the rest of humanity might be they are still a part of it.

> [The cave] sheltered us and brought us to know ourselves and chose the only way of peace. . . . I am grateful for that harsh instruction because it taught us wisdom and gave us happiness beyond fear and thought of our own safety.

With this sense of renewed involvement and hope the novel could have ended, but Macpherson's austere vision takes the story further, and the book ends with the deaths of Terry and Hugh. The ending is harrowing but inevitable. They had known from the start that they would probably not survive: 'we'll never escape, we'll starve and rot in this den, this hole in the rock'. The tragedy of it is that death is the price they must pay for their new self-awareness. As Terry dies first it is particularly harrowing for Hugh. Losing Terry tests him to the limits of his being because she has comforted and supported him from the start. Terry's faith was always stronger than Hugh's and with her death Hugh's faith in their new awareness, his belief in the value of their life together, is given the ultimate test.

When he stalks and kills the men who had killed Terry, Hugh is acting in a very human way but he is also going against everything she had tried to teach him. In 'savouring' this revenge he seems simply to be continuing the violence which Terry had so wanted to end. Aiming at the last man, Hugh is stopped by a vision of Terry which appears in front of him: 'Her eyes gazed at me, her outstretched arms pleaded'. He cannot shoot and, as he throws down his rifle, he is shot and fatally wounded. It seems that at the end he passes the test and affirms his love for Terry by dying for her and what she believes in. His faith was harder-won but perhaps because of that it is even stronger. The book thus ends with an affirmation of the human spirit and a refusal to demean it by the use of violence against others. It is a lesson mankind still has to learn.

Wild Harbour is very different from Macpherson's other novels,[2] but with its marvellous and moving evocation of light and landscape, its detailed descriptions of the process of stalking, and the accuracy and realism of its picture of a life lived out of doors and in direct contact with the elements, it is still a very Scottish novel. Writers like Stevenson in _Kidnapped_, and Crockett in _The Raiders_ had explored similar territory before Macpherson and it is a territory in which the Scottish novelist seems particularly at home, with novels like Buchan's _Sick Heart River_ and Neil Gunn's _Bloodhunt_ being part of the same tradition. That alone, of course, does not make _Wild Harbour_ a classic. That comes from the way Macpherson has created, out of an essentially very simple central situation, a novel imbued with a deep and haunting apprehension of man's precarious position in the universe. Sadly that insight was underlined by Macpherson's own early death in a motorcycle accident in 1944 which surely robbed Scottish literature of a writer of great promise and originality of vision.

John Burns

NOTES TO INTRODUCTION

1. Donald Campbell, introduction to 1981 reprint of _Wild Harbour_, p. vi.
2. For short accounts of Macpherson's other works see John R. Allan, _The North-East Lowlands of Scotland_ (1952), pp. 180–182, and Cuthbert Graham, 'Ian Macpherson: a neglected pastoral novelist', _The Weekend Scotsman_, January 19, 1980, p. 4.

THIS MORNING I said to Terry, 'I thought I heard guns through the night.'

'Were you awake too?' she asked.

Even before she spoke, as soon as the words were out of my mouth I was sorry I spoke, and hastened to say:

'That was funny, both of us lying quiet not to disturb the other.' I knew by the way she looked at me that she was not deceived.

'They sounded very near,' she said; 'in the direction of Inverness.'

'Oh, I don't know,' I returned. 'With this east wind it's very hard to tell how far away sounds are. I remember in nineteen-eighteen we used to hear the guns in France, often on a Sunday morning, if the wind was right, so near and clear you'd think they were close by. We knew when a battle was coming on by the noise, swelling out of the east like a heavy sea. Lord, what an age ago that seems! We didn't know each other then, Terry. How old were you? Seven? I was eight when the War finished, Gone eight, I used to say, bigsy, you know, making a grown-up of myself. But I can remember the guns and when there was fighting in the North Sea—'

'I heard that too,' she broke in. 'It was always a rumbling noise then, not distinct and separate like last night. Last night's noise resembled the Fleet at gun-practice in the Moray Firth. You know how we used to see the glare and flash in the sky before we heard the sound of the guns. I saw fire in the sky last night, on the horizon over there.'

'Wildfire,' I suggested. 'If it was, I hope we get this place properly tight and snug before the weather breaks.

I

You always see wildfire when a storm's brewing in the hills.'

'I hope it was wildfire,' she said after a brief silence, and then: 'I'm going to start spring-cleaning.'

I began to laugh and say something about Nero, but she interrupted me angrily.

'You know how important it is for us to keep a grip on ourselves,' she cried; 'even if we *are* fugitives in a cave—all the more because of that. We daren't let ourselves grow careless. It might be all right to lounge and laze just now while the weather's good, but if we get into a slovenly way we'll never get out of it, and by winter we'll be savages, dirty and cold and demoralized. It wasn't to degenerate into savages that we came here.'

'No,' I said moodily; 'we had a lot of good reasons, but they don't look so good now. Och, Terry, don't heed me. I'm sorry, I shouldn't have said that. I don't mean it really. Only when I see ourselves making ourselves at home here, and settling down as if for ever, I feel it's going to be for ever. That sets me wondering what's happening, if anything's happening, or if we ran away from nothing at all but our own imaginations.'

'The *noise* wasn't wildfire,' she answered. 'I wish I could find an occupation to keep your mind busy, boy. I've got *my* job thinking out meals and how to economize our stores—why don't you write?'

'Write!' I exclaimed. 'Good God, is that what you'd like me to do? Didn't you hear the guns last night, don't you know the whole world's in a flame? What'll I write, now; fairy-tales maybe for cities drowned in gas, or shall I scribe moralities on the rock with a nail for future generations to wonder at my wisdom?'

'You needn't be so hasty to take me up wrongly,' she protested. 'What I was going to say was that you could write an account of the things that happen to us, about our coming here and living here. If we get out of hiding other folk might be glad to know how we lived, and if no

one cares except ourselves, we shall be glad of something
to keep us in mind of the past.'

'Shall we need written mementoes for that?' I asked
bitterly. 'Oh, I think you could find a better occupation
than that for me, Terry, something useful, like counting
the clouds, if I'm too idle. Or I could take a hammer and
break down rocks to dust—or go to the succour of my
king and country—'

'Hush! hush!' she entreated. 'We came here because
we thought it was right, because we would not be bullied into
doing wrong or assisting at wickedness. If we commence to
doubt that—'

'What cures doubt?' I demanded.

'Faith,' she replied simply, 'and my work in this place.
Do you think, Hugh, it's easy for me to plan spring-cleaning
when I know the world's in agony?'

She turned to carry stuff from the back of the cave to the
entrance, now sunlit and warm, for the clouds had passed
from the morning sky.

'That will soon dry out any damp,' she said with
satisfaction. 'Look, Hugh, do you remember when we
made up these?'

She showed me some notebooks and scraps of paper.

'What is it?' I asked. 'The lists we made! listen to
this, Terry, "syrup, treacle, lard"; how much of that have
we? What a hope we had to imagine we'd fetch everything
we needed to make life comfortable into this place. It's a
wonder we didn't mark down a kitchen range.'

'We didn't *quite* bring everything we hoped to bring,' she
agreed.

'It seems years ago, in another world. It was in another
world. We were children playing at desert islands.'

'Oh fine Crusoes! We didn't rightly believe that war
would come. Catch! they'll be useful for lighting the fire
some morning when we forget to dry heather. As if we were
plotting a picnic! Lovely picnic!'

'Has it been so *very* dreadful, Hugh? I'd never dream
of burning them. The excitement we had when we made

them! and you'd come running every now and then to tell me something we'd forgotten—opening the kitchen door and spoiling my baking.'

'Aren't you going to burn them?' I asked. 'I thought you were spring-cleaning and getting rid of rubbish.'

'Must you go on hurting me?' she asked suddenly.

'I didn't mean to hurt you,' I said miserably. 'Oh, Terry, I'm sorry.'

'It's all right, now,' she replied. 'I felt low for a minute. I thought I might be a bother to you, or getting on your nerves. You're not angry because I want to do spring-cleaning, are you, Hugh?

'I knew this was bound to happen,' she said a little later. 'We were too exalted these past weeks.'

'It was such fine weather,' I said, 'and now there's an east wind.'

'It was lovely weather; but Hugh, we must keep a note of what happens.'

'For the foxes to read when they've their den to themselves again?' I asked with renewed bitterness.

'For ourselves to read, and other people, when this is all over.'

'What if it's never all over and we crouch here till we die, and the world goes back to savagery—have you thought of how it'll be when we grow too old to skulk and hide and make shifts and stalk deer for to-morrow's dinner? Shall we come to thrive on grass and heather, or simply starve—what heart can I have for writing?'

'If you were crouching in a trench, Hugh, in wet and mud, and I was crouching in a cellar waiting for the sound of aeroplanes, and bad news—you'd have a certainty that we'd both crouch there for ever—and help the world back to savagery. If you're unhappy here and hankering to go, you hurt me more by staying. I'm not going with you. I can't chop and change my mind every time there's water in the wind. I came here and here I stay until the world changes its mind, for I'll not change mine.'

'What is there to write,' I asked, 'except the days of the

week, and you mark that? Nothing happens; I haven't a
pencil—'

'I have pencil and paper too,' she began in a matter-of-fact
voice. But her voice trembled and she exclaimed, 'I hope
nothing ever happens!' and then she commenced to laugh
and cry alternately, saying, 'Hugh, I couldn't bear to lose
you, I couldn't live without you, I'd sooner be dead. You
won't leave me ever, will you? I don't care what happens
to the world if I have you.'

I suppose I cried too, for the civilization that brought us
to exile had first unfitted us for the life of outlaws. When
that May storm was past we stood together in the mouth of
the cave. The wind had fallen and the sun shone, altering
the tumbled desolation round us from the appearance it bore
while the east wind blew. Nesting grouse called in the valley,
and an early deer calf, high in its lair in a corrie, lamented
its hunger and its absent mother.

'If we could sleep winter through—' I sighed.

'We have all summer to make ready in,' Terry answered.
'We'll manage without sleeping, Hugh. Haven't we peats
and bog-fir and a store of matches?'

'What am I going to write?' I asked.

'Write,' she bade me, 'how we saw war coming. And war
came. Write that we would not be militarized nor suffer
the shame and injuries people would put on us for hating
war. Tell how we left our house by night. Soon we'll have
enough grouse feathers to make a feather-bed, and our peats
are ready for stacking—'

'Yes!' I cried, infected by her enthusiasm; 'and we
made stuff to pickle eggs, and built a wall at the end of
the cave—'

'A million things to write,' she said. 'Here's a pencil;
put it all down every single thing we did.'

So I took a notebook in one hand and my telescope in the
other, and slung my little rifle over my shoulder in case a
grouse or hare came within range since we could not afford
to let slip a single chance of getting food, though it was
breeding-time and I was loath to kill. When I had spied to

make sure that the country was vacant except for ourselves and birds and beasts I sat down in the lee of a great stone, warmed and illumined by the midday sun, and began to recall how we came into the hills, while Terry put water in a basin to clean the rocky cavern where we hid.

It was strange, but as I tried to recall the past which was so near in point of days, I found that the past, distant and near, was faint and scarcely to be recalled. Things no more than a month old, the fret and confusion of our escape which I thought was indelibly marked on my memory, proved suddenly as insubstantial and dispersed as the puffs of mist which float across a sunlit morning hill, dappled by clouds and sun. I could remember many times when Terry and myself said, 'We'll never forget this to our dying day,' and the fact of the event which made us speak so was clear enough in my memory, but I could not feel it. These old events seemed like things I had been told, and heard with a vagrant mind.

I looked round the wild empty scene; it had its terrors, winter, and storm, sudden cliffs and green bogs, but they were not such as fretted the humanity we had fled from; no sign of man or man's handiwork save a distant fence and burnt patches of heather on the moor was there to remind us of the man-made horror we had left behind us. Yet a mere month ago we were the fools of rumour, a prey to whispers, racked by fear and loathing. To-day the sun shone. We lived in the remote world which is not divided from men by miles alone; a greater distance than the rough hill barriers divided us from our kind; the callous earth, unchanged in war and pestilence, occupied time as if there were no men, and we lived there, in that strict country.

The wind abating to a breath lulled me. Even the brief unhappiness of the morning, which owed to the east wind, faded into the past, and I should soon have been asleep had not a movement on the hill-slope facing us taken my eye. I had reached a state of continual unconscious vigilance. Quite automatically, with my mind still turned backwards, I took my glass from its case and rubbed the lenses with

my handkerchief and looked towards the facing hill. I saw
a herd of deer, twenty or thirty stags with the new horn just
visible, milling uneasily. They rushed now in one direction,
now in the other. The wind though light was steady. It was
impossible they could have seen me at the distance. I had
not moved enough to attract their attention and I had taken
care to blacken the brass of my telescope so that it should not
shine in the sun and betray me. Once, long ago, I had been
saved from a gamekeeper who tried to catch me poaching
because I saw his telescope gleaming in the heather, and
it taught me a lesson. Anxiety commenced to replace my
beatific calm, until I heard Terry speak. She was standing
at the door of the cave shaking out a deer-skin.

'Isn't it the loveliest *lovely* day!' she cried.

'Terry!' I retorted, 'what on earth are you doing, standing
there? Don't you know to be more careful? Lie down and
keep quite still.'

It was amusing to see the sudden change that came on
her face, and the haste with which she flung herself on the
ground, not even waiting to make sure that the place she
chose was dry or smooth. She lay for a few seconds in
absolute silence. Then she raised her head with exaggerated
caution to peer about her, dropping her head almost as soon
as she lifted it.

'Ostrich!' I murmured.

'Can I come up, Hugh?' she whispered. At my nod she
crawled and dragged herself to where I waited.

'Did I do right?' she inquired anxiously. 'Is there any
one? Was I bad? You were only giving me a fright!'
Her startled eyes reproached me.

'All the deer in the country were watching you,' I stated.

She breathed her relief and sat up laughing.

'I thought for certain some one had seen me. My heart
came into my mouth. What would we do if it had been a
man, Hugh?'

'Leave here and find another hiding-place,' I told her
grimly.

'Leave our cave! We couldn't do that, after the work

we've done. What a fright I got. My heart's going like a jakey mill. It doesn't matter for deer.'

'It might, Terry. They should be lying at peace just now, and if a gamekeeper saw stags running away from this direction a few times he'd soon grow suspicious. It's not the deer seeing us that matters but other people seeing the deer. Lie down and let them settle.'

'I should be working,' she protested feebly. 'What a gorgeous day! Who'd imagine there was trouble in the world?' She crouched low in the heather.

'Och, no need to lie so close as that,' I laughed. 'So long as you don't go moving abruptly there's no fear. Stags haven't very good eyes and the sun's against them. That's a pretty noticeable jersey you're wearing.'

'Don't you like it?' she asked, wide-eyed. 'I thought it suited me.'

'You know, Terry,' I continued, 'the biggest danger we have to contend with is that we'll become too contented here and give up all thought of the future.'

'I like being contented,' she returned.

'It's not easy to believe that men are killing each other,' I went on.

'How is the diary going?' she asked. I showed her the blank pages of the notebook.

'Terry,' I said, 'when we were so miserable, only a month past, I thought I'd never escape remembering.'

'It was an unhappy time, Hugh.'

'I'd never like to go through a time like it again. But Terry, it's as if it never happened for all I can feel of it now. Like a dream, or a tale in a book, or old gossip. I can scarcely believe there was a time when we weren't here. This country seems the only reality, and you can't feel with your heart that the affairs of men are important; it's hard to believe there are men, in a country so empty, so self-sufficient, as this.'

'A woeful dream, if it was a dream,' she whispered. 'A dream that murders men. Maybe this forgetting defends us.'

'Against—madness,' I took her up soberly. 'We were

walking on a thin edge, Terry, when we were so uncertain and divided in our minds.'

'We were lucky,' she said. 'A great many couldn't have lived here, even if they had the opportunity. If you hadn't learned to poach—'

'If we hadn't been poor—' I went on. 'It's queer to be lucky by force of hard circumstances. If we hadn't been forced to poach, and dig bog-fir, and make shifts because we hadn't money to buy meat and coal and comforts we couldn't have lasted a week here.'

'You'd imagine things were shaped for a purpose,' she agreed. 'It was complete chance that made us find this cave. A thunderstorm—'

'And bad temper,' I said, and laughed.

'I remember finding it; I remember as if it was yesterday,' she said in a ruminative voice. 'Oh my, we were wet and cross and miserable! The midges almost ate us alive. When was it, nineteen-thirty-two, twelve years ago.'

We had gone fishing for pike on Loch Coulter, a tarn which lies a mile off the road between Dalwhinnie and Laggan Bridge and now shines beneath us to the east of our home. In the afternoon a thunderstorm came over. We hauled our boat ashore and walked up a gorge westwards in the direction of Ardverikie Forest and the high hills, looking for shelter and a place where we could kindle a fire and boil our kettle. Each boulder that tempted us to halt had another more tempting shelter-stone a few yards above it. We were at that stage between dry clothes and sopping when the pelting open seems preferable to a refuge which merely slows down the rate at which one grows wet and we clambered dismally from one inadequate covert to another up the steep north side of the ravine. I think there is iron in the cliffs which overhang that slope. Flashes of lightning dazzled us, so near we heard them crack like whips, and thunder reverberated amongst the peaks with scarcely a pause. Under that great sound the rising streams grumbled and rain beat on the earth.

A cloud of midges drove us half frantic and we climbed higher to escape them, though we carried them with us, through heather two foot long, over screes and gravel slides. We were soaked to the skin long before we discovered the cave, beneath a bulge of cliff. It was not strictly a cave. An immense slab of rock had fallen from the precipice. At the foot of the cliff it tumbled inwards to lean against the parent mass from which it broke away, making a long narrow tent open at both ends. Rubble had accumulated along the ridge. Heather took hold in it, and tough grass interspersed with tiny rowan trees wove a matted thatch which kept out the rain. It was dark and cold in the cave but since we had found what we were searching for we were perversely determined to make use of it in spite of the fact that we would have been warmer, and could not have become wetter, in the open.

The storm passed and we crawled out of the cave to sun ourselves and view the scene.

'Would this be one of Prince Charlie's caves?' Terry wanted to know.

'He passed this way to Benalder,' I told her, 'so no doubt it would be a Prince Charlie cave if people knew about it.'

'But why don't people know?' she continued. 'I'm sure there are dozens of places far more remote and wild than this and you can scarcely get near them for hikers and sightseers.'

'No one comes this way,' I explained, 'not even a game-keeper. There's very little game; too many ravens and foxes and wild cats in this tangle of rock, and eagles from Benalder hunt here. Look, over there, under the Farrow, you can see the head of the Durc, where the eagles nest. Besides, it's a sort of dead corner with narrow angles of half a dozen moors and forests meeting. Each angle by itself is too small to be worth shooting. As for hikers, there's nothing majestic or romantic here, nothing but empty desolation.'

'I like it,' she declared. 'Well, we have our cave in No Man's Land, Hugh. What a place to hide in! like the Macgregors had, for desperate outlaws!'

'In summer,' I agreed. 'What are you looking for?'

'Things. Rock-drawings and flint arrow-heads.'

'Fox's dung more likely, and stinking bones.'

'Don't be cruel, Hugh,' she retorted. 'Now if you walled

up one end the cave would be very snug. I'm sure people have lived in much worse places.'

'What food would there be?' I asked scornfully. 'You can't grow things here. What about the snowdrift? Were you thinking of flitting up here, Terry?'

How bitterly our jests reproach us when the thing we mocked comes to pass. I answered myself eleven years later, in 1943, when war was in all our mouths, and daily rumours shook the world. We had never revisited the cave. We had spoken about it only once, to one man, a stalker who lived near our house and came often on a winter night to play draughts and recall the war in France where he had fought for four years. But wherever the conversation began, it always ended with Duncan telling us that we were degenerate compared with our ancestors.

'You don't require to talk to me, Hugh,' he declared dogmatically one evening in the summer of 1943; we were sitting before our house smoking and watching dusk hide the village of Newtonmore.

'You know as well as I do that folk to-day couldn't live on what made their fathers as strong as giants,' he went on vehemently. 'Take any man in a town and put him out here in the hills to live by himself and he wouldn't last a week. A week! not two days.'

'That's not fair,' Terry argued. 'You can't take a man in a town and compare him with country folk of old.'

'Take a man in the country, then,' Duncan persisted. 'Take myself, take Hugh. If we were forced to live by our own efforts, how'd we thrive? It stands to reason we couldn't do it. Our senses are blunted. We depend on a multitude of people to make our clothes and food and tools for us. We have noses that can't smell, ears that are deaf—'

'Nevertheless we have intelligence,' I stated.

'Brains don't keep you warm,' he declared.

'But they do,' I went on. 'And though we haven't the noses of deer nor the eyes of eagles, we hunt deer and capture eagles. All the same, you're asking too much, Duncan. Why, your very wild beasts, your deer for instance, can scarcely survive a winter, a bad winter, amongst these hills without artificial feeding. You give them bruised oats and Indian corn, don't you?'

'They're degenerate too,' he retorted.

'It's comparatively simple for men to live the savage life or like Robinson Crusoe in tropical fertile countries, Duncan,' I continued. 'Speed and strength and alert senses wouldn't avail a man much if he were flung out into the Grampians to live by what he could kill and grow. He'd die, pretty soon, however savage and undegenerate he was.'

We drifted into discussing how long one could survive the climate, the cold and hunger, of the mountainous north, if one were left entirely to one's own devices for food and shelter, clothing and fire. We agreed that without a great many tools and stores of clothing and such things as salt, one would die soon.

'And when your ammunition was all used up,' Duncan jibed, 'where would you find shelter?'

'There's shelter waiting in a cave in the rock above Loch Coulter,' I said. 'With a little work it could be made warm and tight. There are tons of peats and fir roots waiting to be dug just beside it. You could learn to use a bow and arrow. You could catch pike.'

'How would you avoid scurvy?' Terry asked. 'Would you dig a garden? Where would you get seeds? As far as I can see you would require pots and pans and dishes and needles and thread—'

'And a furniture removal van,' Duncan laughed.

We laughed with him. How easy it was to make a joke then. To laugh now is to raise apprehension in our minds, for so many things that we smiled to think on have come true, have come true and no jest.

'Trust the housewife,' I lamented. 'If ever you think of living the savage life, Duncan, consult Terry.'

'Oh, I don't think it's impossible,' she protested. 'It would be a dreadful life, but one could live. After all, Hugh, we ourselves require very little to keep us alive except clothing and flour and salt, and we could manage with less. We grow vegetables, we dig peats.'

'If living's all,' I said.

'If living's all.'

I used to think that these years of rumour, when war loomed, could never be remembered save with pain. Yet as I regard that decade, to-day, I wonder that I ever endured them, not because they were unhappy, but because they were futile and wearisome. I feel that custom alone made us live amongst the fears and murmurs of storm, and deferred our escape.

We started to speak once more about our cave in the autumn of 1943.

'You were in France,' I said to Duncan. 'You've seen—' I paused as a new thought came to my head. 'Duncan,' I said, 'did you know—did you ever know that you killed any one?'

He turned his dark-lined melancholy face towards the horizon of the Monadhliahs and kept silent until I began to think I had said what I should not.

'Once,' he said, in a low voice, 'the Jerries were coming over in the dawn, but light enough to see the sights of your rifle, a surprise attack, no guns, no noise, nothing but them—and us.'

He paused a moment.

'You know how it is when you've lived with a gun in your hand as I've done,' he appealed to me. 'The sights come in line afore you know it—I had a bead on a Jerry. He was dead, Hugh, as sure as God I had him dead like the hind I got last week, before ever I pulled the trigger. I couldn't do it, I couldn't do it.' His voice grew harsh.

'Likely some one else did,' he said.

'Not you,' Terry whispered.

'Would you go back?' I asked, after a while. 'Yes?'

'Yes. We'd not be asked,' he said in heavy tones. 'We'd be conscripted. Well,'—he shrugged his shoulders,—'every man has it coming to him some time.'

'Conscripted? Good God!' I cried, 'would you go for

that? They'd call me up amongst the first. I wouldn't go.'

'It's easy to say that now.'

'Why should you be called up, Hugh?' Terry inquired in a strained voice.

'Oh, having been in the Terriers.' I avoided her eyes. 'I think you swear to take up arms in defence of your king and country.'

'You'd go?' Her voice had the horror of death.

'We wouldn't be asked,' Duncan explained.

'Christ, I wouldn't go,' I said in a rage. 'No, nor I wouldn't be flung in jail and beaten and abused, neither. I'll tell you what I'd do, I'd take a rifle and plenty of ammunition and hide amongst the hills, and if they wanted me they could come and take me, but not alive.'

'Back to your cave, Hugh,' Duncan said.

'Any place would do me,' I rushed on. 'Oh, I'd fight all right, I'm no pacifist when it comes to defending my own right, but I'll not fight in any bloody stupid war. War's not fun any longer; it's murder, and I'm not a murderer.'

'You'd be a lot safer and more comfortable in the army, Hugh,' Duncan declared. 'You might get a cushy job. Better than lying out on the hill, cold and hungry, scared of every sound and move.'

'Half an hour ago you were praising the men of old for lying out on the hill,' I told him.

'*They* could do it.'

'So can I, and so I shall,' I answered wildly. 'I saw as much of the army as I want and I've heard enough of war from you to know I won't take part in it. Better starve and shiver than be a frightened slave.'

When Duncan went away Terry said, 'I didn't know you'd been a Territorial, Hugh.'

'I was a stupid young fool,' I told her shortly.

'But why?' she wanted to know. 'It's not the sort of thing I'd imagine attracting you.'

'I was hard up and a crowd of us fancied the holiday. You get five pounds for attending the summer camp.'

'My little mercenary! Were you a good soldier, Hugh?'

'No, I was not. I don't want to hear more about it. I told you I was a young fool.'

'How in the world did you let yourself be disciplined?' she persisted.

'I didn't,' I admitted wryly. 'It was all so damned stupid. It revolted me. After all, I was good material. I could shoot, I had hit living moving things, which was more than most of the other men had done or would ever do. I had trained eyes, I knew how to take advantage of cover. But because I didn't wear my kilt just so, and polish my buttons properly, the best they could do with me was make me clean out lavatories, shovelling filth to learn the art of war.'

'Poor Hugh!'

'If there was any sign of intelligence in the business a man could take pride in doing it well, even though he knew it was a bad business at the best. But to charge in a bunch over open country with fixed bayonets and horses galloping, in the year nineteen-twenty-eight, as if the Great War was a myth! If I had a rifle with decent sights I could have killed most of the whole army. Duncan uses an army .303 for the hinds; they're fine weapons, dead true and practically flat up to a couple of hundred yards. *He* put on leaf sights. All you have to do is flick a leaf up or down when you're changing your range. That's not difficult enough for the army. The army doesn't want good, simple, workman-like sights. What's not good enough for killing deer is quite sufficient for defending your life and your country. And that's only one example of how much they learn from experience. Maybe wars are justified sometimes. They used to have a sort of justification before they became too big and dreadful for any justification. Justified or not, they're a stupid way of settling things, and as far as I ever saw, stupidly run.'

'They'd call you up?' she asked a little later.

'Right away,' I agreed.

'I think you'd go.' Her voice was harsh.

'I would not.' I was angry with everything, even with her.

'You say that now. When the pipes begin to play and all your friends to leave—'

'And all the neighbours to point at me and the little boys to throw stones at me—say it, Terry! God in Christ, don't you think it's difficult enough already for me to believe I'm right? *Must* you make it worse, disbelieving me?'

'It's going to be war,' men said in the winter of that year. 'War,' I said, when Terry heard the whispers and the words which swelled through our quiet valley. She turned her back on me and walked to the window and stared out over the valley, white from the black Spey's edge to the far scarp of the Monadhliahs.

'Terry!' I implored, going to her and turning her to face me. Tears ran down her white cheeks like rain. 'Terry, you mustn't grieve; my dear, you mustn't grieve.'

'So many men to kill and kill and die, what makes grief quiet?' she cried wildly.

'If I could see, if I could see clearly!' I cried. 'I've no doubt it's easy for some folk to believe that war's wrong. All the instincts I ever got are for trouble, and intellectual persuasion's cold comfort when it's against one's instincts. Oh, Terry, I don't think I could bear to live in this country, where we know everyone, where we are friendly with every one, if war came, for I'm not going to fight, and there'd be nothing but contempt and mockery for us.'

'People have changed since the last war,' she declared without much conviction.

'Do you believe that?' I asked. 'Do you believe that the people who beat and jailed pacifists in the last war will be any kinder in the next?'

'No,' she said, and then, 'Hugh, what are we going to do?'

'If only I could see—'

'They shan't take you,' she said fiercely. 'We'll go away from here. To suffer humiliation, to be a criminal in the eyes of every one—'

'Even myself. Where can we escape that?'

And in a little time the dark future became the present.

'They won't shame us,' I said harshly. 'We're not their

clowns to beat and spit at. I'll take you to your people, Terry.'

'And you, what will you do?' she asked aghast.

'I'll go where they won't get me; or if they do, it'll cost them blood.'

'Hugh!'

'If you'd rather me be flung into prison and labelled a coward, because I won't be involved in murder and outrage—'

'I'll go too.'

'Better to hide with the fox,' I went on drearily.

'I go where you go,' she said.

'Have you forgotten what Duncan told you?'

'I forget everything except that I won't leave you. Hugh, would you really send me away?' she asked, trying to laugh. 'Who'd mend your clothes, and wash the dishes, and tell you where to find things? Oh! oh! my heart will break.' She wept and sobbed in my arms.

'Hush, hush, my love,' I besought her. 'Don't you understand? I'd be a fugitive, hiding from all the world in the roughest hills, listening for footsteps in every wind, starting at my shadow—'

She shook her head violently.

'I can hide too, and skulk in the rocks,' she said. 'I'm not afraid of anything except losing you . . .

'I'm all right now, Hugh,' she went on. 'I'm sorry—for a minute the world was dark, no light in all the earth, nothing but dark, dark, fearful dark. We must be calm! We must make plans, and be ready. Could we really live in that cave, Hugh?'

'It would be rough—' I began.

'Who cares for roughness!' she returned angrily. 'I'm not so weak that I must be nursed, Hugh, and kept from hearing the truth, like a fool or a child.'

'I'm sorry, Terry,' I said humbly. 'Other people have lived in caves, hermits and robbers and fugitives from tyrants—what fools we'll feel if there's no need to go.'

'What does it matter, then? You know as well as I do that war is coming.'

'You don't believe that I'm a coward?' I asked anxiously.

'I don't think so, Hugh,' she replied with a pale smile.

'To be killed is nothing so dreadful,' I went on, 'if a man can see a just cause for dying. I think I could suffer pain—mutilation—'

'For God's sake stop!' she cried in a shrill voice. Her eyes were wild and her face was haggard.

'It's this madness, this war, it kills and kills, and when the killing's done, all that it accomplishes is to set the stage for more.' I could not stop. I could not cease from speaking and tormenting myself with horror.

'How much money have we?' she asked with an effort to control her speech.

I looked at my pass-book.

'Fifty-three pounds,' I said.

'I don't think we should let our minds prey on things,' she said. She drew a deep breath. The colour returned to her cheeks. 'We believe that we are doing right. We aren't willing to be mocked and ill-used and made the butt of fools and ruffians for doing right. Isn't it simple?'

'We should be willing—' I said.

'Yes.'

'We must arrange, we must think out the smallest details,' she continued. 'We have fifty-three pounds to spend.'

'I'll buy as much ammunition for the .22 as my permit will let me have,' I declared. 'It won't be wasted at any rate, even if we stay at home.'

'Stay at home!' she broke in. 'We'll be leaving our house! Hugh, I never thought of that! we were happy in it.'

So we began to make our plans, to write down lists of what we would require, if we were to live in hiding, in the hills, out of reach of our enemies. The occupation of planning our life, away from the hazards and ills of common life, freed us to a certain extent from our preoccupation with these ills. While we were making lists of food and tools and clothing the threat of war receded a little, so that when our lists were completed, and we were in imagination already escaped, the immediate necessity for escape was no longer there to urge us to action, though Terry was anxious to begin buying those things we needed most.

But I grew loath, as time wore on and rumours became a commonplace of our lives, to spend our money against a contingency which might never arise.

'I have a feeling there won't be a war,' I argued when Terry reproached me. 'Surely people have more sense by this time of day. Besides, war doesn't come out of a clear sky. We'll have warning in ample time.'

'So will other people, and prices will rise,' she said. 'Have you bought your ammunition?'

'Yes. It's not like flour and sugar and such perishables. It will keep indefinitely and one always finds use for it.'

'How much?'

'Five thousand rounds for the .22, all my permit allows. Five hundred for the .303. I had to pay through the nose for that, since I haven't a permit.'

We put off buying provisions until spring came. Our fears were slowly allayed, not only by the apathy which comes when one has made ready to face a difficulty which fails to appear, but also by a changed tone in the world's affairs.

'And all our worry and plans were wasted,' I said to Terry in early March. 'I'm going to begin digging the garden.'

'Not wasted, Hugh,' she reproached me. 'The fate that makes our worry vain is too happy for grudging.'

'I am almost sorry we aren't to go,' I went on, teasing her. 'We would have enjoyed being cave-dwellers.'

'Oh hush, Hugh!' she cried. 'I won't let you speak like that.'

I started to dig the garden and to buy seeds. On the third of April we went fishing on Loch Ericht. We brought a nice basket of trout home in the evening.

'I'll light the stove if you clean the trout,' Terry told me. 'Turn on the wireless until we hear the weather report. If it's to be fine to-morrow we'll go for a picnic to Fortwilliam, maybe. I'm longing for the sea.'

'Terry!' I shouted, when I heard the first words the loudspeaker gave forth. 'Terry!'

She came running from the kitchen with the frying-pan in her hand. We stood in front of the wireless, as if we heard our doom spoken by its inanimate voice. We were on the brink of war. The nations were mobilizing. War, war, war. Across the continent we heard that sound. Cheering crowds, hoarse orators, marching feet, drums and babel.

'Shut it off,' Terry said. It was there still.

'I never dreamt of this; that it would come to this,' she breathed.

'I should have known!' I cried in an agony of self-reproach.

'We must see how much we have in the house,' she said. 'I'll go out immediately and buy everything I can get.'

'I doubt if you'll get anything,' I told her. 'We'll be rationed right away. It's too late to get money from the bank. Why did I delay?'

'Some one will cash a cheque, Hugh.'

'What are we going to do, Terry?'

'Do? what we made up our minds to do. What else?'

'We counted on stores and tools.'

She went out to return in an hour with a burden of small parcels.

'I got a little here and there,' she said breathlessly. 'The place is mad, Hugh, bonfires, shouting, guns going off—'

We sat at our door until late, until after midnight, surveying the village with its bonfires, man's funeral pyre.

Two days later, on the fifth of April, Terry brought in an official envelope from the post.

'I won't, I won't!' I cried in a rage.

'Let's sit down and think matters over calmly,' Terry said. 'What—what does it say?'

I tore the envelope open.

'It gives me two days,' I answered. 'Two days!'

'And after that?'

'Well, if I don't appear—' I made a motion to indicate manacled hands.

'We must go at once,' she said.

We went through the house, picking out all we counted we'd need, and reading through our lists as we searched. By nightfall the kitchen floor was piled with parcels and tins and boxes and bundles of clothing. The house already wore a gutted look. In the dusk I could see Terry's pale face, drawn and weary, but with eyes that showed no yielding to weariness or doubt. I brought our baby car to the door.

'We'll load as much as we can into the car, Terry,' I said, 'and take it up by the Glentruim road until we get as near as possible to Loch Coulter. Then we'll dump the stuff and I'll carry it to the cave while darkness lasts. You'll come here again with the car. To-morrow you'll go to Kingussie, anywhere you can buy food. To-morrow night at ten I'll be waiting in the same place as we'll find to-night.'

We were but young in stealth. As we drove along the Spey, towards Loch Coulter, the silent night was full of ears that harkened to our passing. We laboured up the hill from the Spey, by Cattlodge with its crofts and staring windows and human folk in another world from us. It was midnight when our second journey ended, and dark, dark.

'I'll be waiting here for you to-morrow night,' I told Terry. 'Go home and sleep, my dear, you'll need all your sleep.'

'Oh, my dear!' she cried, 'how can I leave you here alone! Hugh, Hugh, this dreadful night—'

'This night makes us free,' I murmured, little feeling free.

I made heavy progress with my loads through the mire and stones to Loch Coulter. Stumbling and falling, saving my precious luggage at the expense of my hands and knees, I went back and fore, half-asleep though I kept a straight course. We had not thought about making the parcels easy to carry; we had omitted to wrap things that would break in blankets or clothing to protect them. I had even forgotten to leave food unwrapped and easy to get at. At length cock-grouse, whose wings I had heard many a time when I disturbed them in the gloom, commenced to hail the approach of day. Our stuff was hidden safely amongst heather in a jungle of young birch at the head of Loch

Coulter. It was impossible to carry it to the cave in darkness
and when light came I was too tired to lift another burden.
I dragged myself up the hill to the cave with a couple of
blankets and a dry loaf. I was too tired to eat. I was too
tired to sleep. Yet I did not wake. The moist dark cavern
lightened from the east, and the sun rose, and reached the
south, and went down, while I lay waiting.

Terry came to the meeting-place at ten o'clock.

'We must hurry,' I said. 'We have to get rid of the car. I
hope it won't be as dark as it was last night. I put my feet in
every hole between here and Loch Coulter. Could you drive
the car to Dalwhinnie and up the side of Loch Ericht until
you find a steep place, and run it over into the loch? That
would hide it safely. Then walk back here and wait for me,
if I'm not already waiting.'

'You're wet, you're shivering,' she said. 'When had you
food last? I'm not going to leave you, Hugh; I'm staying
with you.'

I was loath to send her away from me again, and I agreed
that we could hide the car in a gravel pit for two or three days.
There might be things on it which would prove useful, once
we had time to look about us.

Although we had less to carry this night we were both
dead-beat. The nervous excitement and the anger which had
goaded us so far were failing; we trudged in leaden gloomy
silence, lacking energy even to speak when we tripped over
tussocks, or walked into bogs. Yet, bereft of elation and
anger as we were, weariness itself seemed to carry us on.
Like men in despair who may as well struggle forward as
yield, we laboured on our journeys; the dawn came in grey
and misty; we could hear, but not see, water flowing to the
loch, and waking birds.

'The mist is lucky for us,' I told Terry when our final load
was carried to the head of the loch. 'If you go and make a
fire beside the cave I'll fetch up as much as I can before
the mist rises.' She preferred to help me so that we could
rest without worrying because all our belongings were not
in safety. The fortunate clouds kept low until ten o'clock,

enabling us to complete our task. At length we could see
an end to our flight. I huddled over the fire, wrapped in
blankets, while Terry spread out my wet clothes to dry.
She commenced to hunt through the bundles on the floor.

'Rest, Terry,' I besought her.

'We must have food,' she returned, and gave me the
kettle. I filled it with a cup at the pool beside our cave
which was fed by trickles of water down the rock face.
Terry put fat in the frying-pan; she fried a piece of steak,
with onions, and two eggs, and a slice of bread. So we ate
our first meal in the cave. When it was done I scattered the
fire. We rolled ourselves in blankets and fell asleep on the
ground.

It was a heavy yet troubled sleep I enjoyed, with many
dreams of which vivid fragments persisted into my waking
mind. We wakened at the same time, in the mid-afternoon. I
turned to find Terry watching me with a bewildered childish
expression on her face.

'What is it, Terry?' I asked.

'I had a dream—' she began, and hid her face in her
hands for a moment. When she took them away the baffled
look had gone from her eyes. They were content. I went
out carefully to our pool. She washed herself in the basin
of water I brought, and brushed her hair, talking the while
of what we must do. We made a tally of our goods, piling
them as neatly as possible against the inner wall of the cave
so that we could move freely.

'How long it seems since yesterday,' Terry remarked as
we worked.

'You got a good few things,' I returned.

'Yes, at a price. I had to beg for everything. I went as
far as Inverness. And oh, I worried about you!'

'Poor lassie,' I murmured.

'Then Duncan came. I dared not let him into the house.
He would have known something was wrong if he saw it.
He's been called up. He kept on asking where you were.
Of course he saw the car at the door. I'm sure he thought
you were poaching.'

These were the things we brought with us.

Of clothes, two pairs of shoes besides the pair she was wearing for Terry and two spare pairs of boots for me. We had agreed that it was possible to make garments out of deer-skins if need be, and we had brought nitre and alum to cure skins, but we could not hope to make shoes which would stand wear amongst the rocks and in the heather. We had not grudged to buy the very best. I generally wore shoes, but we decided that boots would keep me drier when I was out hunting food, and that they would save my stockings.

Tackets and rivets and cobbler's twine, and a stout needle to repair our boots and shoes.

A good leather coat each; Terry had a suède jacket as well and I a leather jerkin.

A couple of knitted tams for Terry; two caps and a sou'-wester for me. When we bought our footwear and the ammunition we were afraid our money would not be sufficient to buy new clothes so we determined to use only such as we had in the house. The .303 ammunition cost me six pounds, and the 5,000 rounds for the .22 cost almost eight. We paid practically ten pounds for boots and shoes which left less than thirty pounds to spread over all our other requirements. Of course it proved ample, and we could have bought more, if I had taken Terry's advice to budget exactly and in time. Terry had bought some warm woollen underclothes for herself. When we came away we wore as much as we could to make our parcels less bulky. Terry wore two pairs of stockings, her leather coat and the suède jacket, a jersey and a knitted blouse above her underclothes. I was wearing a khaki shirt, two pull-over jerseys with long sleeves and polo collars, a grey plus-four suit, the jerkin and the leather coat.

Over and above what we wore we had two spare jerseys each; Terry had two Harris tweed jackets and two extra skirts and six or seven pairs of stockings; I had a light strong jacket of cotton and wool, an old tweed jacket, eight pairs of stockings, two pairs of corduroy breeches, a pair of shorts and three khaki shirts. With the exception of the dark brown breeches all my clothes were greys or checks which harmonized with the hill.

We had packed our pockets with small things, needles and thread and several ounces of wool for darning; scissors and a ball of strong twine. Terry produced a set of knitting needles.

'When our knitted things wear through I'll unravel them and reknit them,' she explained.

'If we stay long enough to wear what we've got, it means being here for years,' I said.

'Clothes won't last so long here,' she answered.

We had three double blankets, a ground-sheet, and two dark army blankets to spread over the ground-sheet, underneath us.

Of equal importance with our clothing were our weapons and tools. I had taken great care that they should be good. I had a B.S.A. single shot .22 with Martini action which had often killed a hare at nearly two hundred yards. It had leaf sights for fifty, a hundred, and two hundred yards. I made sure that I got non-fouling rust-preventing ammunition for the .22. The barrel would never rust, nor would it require cleaning. Only too late, when I lifted the .303 from the heap of our stuff, did I realize that I had not brought oil or a ramrod to clean it.

The .303 was an old long Lee-Enfield. I had 500 rounds for it, and I had filed away the noses of the steel-jacketed bullets to make sure that they would spread and kill.

I had a good telescope in a leather case and a pair of cheap binoculars.

I brought also a good sheath-knife for bleeding and skinning deer, and a small oil-stone to sharpen it.

We had fifty rabbit snares all ready made up, and a roll of wire to make more snares.

A hundred yards of flax line for catching pike in Loch Coulter. Treble hooks for pike. Fly and bait hooks for trout; fifty yards of silk line for trout, a gaff, and a net. A spool of artificial gut.

We had a seven-pound axe with a spare handle, a small axe with a hammer head in reverse; files to sharpen them.

A small saw. Cotton rope from Woolworth's. A spade and a kitchen shovel.

Our food was mostly packed in biscuit-tins which we had sealed with brown paper and paste against the damp. We had half a hundredweight of salt in tins. We were worried about salt; it was essential, it was difficult to keep dry, and when it was gone we had no way of getting more. We therefore brought what seemed to ourselves a ridiculously large quantity. It did not appear so large when we began to reflect how useful salted meat would prove.

The same quantity of flour. Two stones of sugar, to be used grudgingly. Two stones of oatmeal for oatcakes. Without fresh milk we did not relish porridge.

We knew we could get plenty of fat from the deer we killed; we brought only two pounds of roast fat and a pound of lard.

Two pounds of baking-powder, a pound of baking-soda, two dozen tins of unsweetened condensed milk and two dozen tins of sweetened. Ten two-pound jars of home-made jam, the remainder of what Terry made on the previous year.

Six pounds of tea, a pound of coffee as an occasional luxury. A stone of salt butter in an earthenware jar. A stone of split peas. To make the beginning of our stay more pleasant Terry had bought six tins of fruit, a box of water biscuits, two dozen fresh eggs, ten pounds of ham in half-pound parcels; she bought them at a dozen different shops; two pounds of frying steak, a stone of carrots, a stone of onions and two loaves of bread. We had a small bag of turnips left over from what our garden grew, and a bag with a hundredweight of potatoes, which almost broke my back when I fetched it to the cave.

We had bought enamelled dishes for picnics in Woolworth's long ago, and we brought them. We packed them in a small bath which would be useful for washing dishes and clothes. We had three soup-plates, three mugs, two small enamelled basins, two good china cups from our own cupboard, four knives and forks and table-spoons and tea-spoons, a ladle and two wooden spoons.

We brought good pans, of cast aluminium or iron, to stand rough usage. We had a large cast aluminium frying-pan and an iron stew-pan, a four-pint aluminium kettle and a gallon iron kettle, an aluminium tea-pot, an iron griddle for baking, a deep iron pan to make soup or for roasting.

A small barrel, packed with tools, would hold water, if there was a drought. We had also a large galvanized iron pail to carry water.

We brought four towels and ten pounds of soap in bars, and an old cotton sheet for washing dishes or making bandages. I had a roll of surgical tape and iodine and a jar of vaseline in my pocket. A bottle of whisky completed our medicine chest.

Amongst the things we forgot to bring were nails, and a wedge to split roots. These at least were missed almost at once. Before we lived long in the cave we discovered many other things we should have taken. But I had alum for skins and saltpetre to make match for flint and steel, if our store of matches ran down.

It was the commonplace necessities we found ourselves most apt to forget. I remembered four pounds of tobacco, but I forgot matches. When I found eight dozen boxes amongst the other stuff I recollected that matches were not on our list, even on the list we made in the easy winter time when we played at planning our life in a cave.

'You *did* remember matches,' I said to Terry. 'If we hadn't matches! The one essential and I forgot all about them.'

'Thank Duncan,' she replied. 'When I saw him, he asked for a match; there wasn't one in the house; I flew to Newtonmore and bought all I could get.'

'We were lucky,' I said with a great breath of relief.

Before night we knew all our store. It seemed a very haphazard collection; we had not reckoned how long we expected to live in the hills, nor suited our purchases to each other so that our necessities would last the same length of time. We were too tired to think. Terry took a sharp stone and scratched on the inner wall of the cave—

April 7, 1944,
and behind the figures she scratched a deep

$$\mathbf{I}$$

'What's that for?' I wanted to know.
'To keep track of the days, We'll make a mark for each day.'
Then we slept again.

WE DO NOT intend this account of our life in hiding to be a strict diary. Days have occurred since we reached here whose passing requires no fuller commemoration than the mark Terry draws every morning on the rock wall of our home. Doubtless many more such days will come to us. Moreover days and hours and the conventional units of time are becoming meaningless. Time is no longer the inflexible system of equal spaces that it was while we lived with our fellows.

For two days after we reached the cave we were spent. We wakened to make food. We slept when we had eaten; like swimmers who have barely escaped with their lives and lie on the shore of the flood that almost swept them away and do not care whether the waters against which they struggled in despair now drag them back, we were overcome with lassitude of mind and body. Freedom, hard-won, tasted stale in our mouths. We savoured nothing, neither our success nor food nor sleep. The dreary waste on which we looked, when we troubled to go to the open air, assumed a hateful aspect.

We revived gradually and painfully. In our hurry to be gone from our house we had had no time to reflect. We were driven by goads whose wounds, scarcely felt when they were inflicted, rankled and festered in these hopeless hours. War and our harsh necessity, the fate of the world, vexed our thoughts and planted venom in our minds.

A very simple emotion finally ousted our discontents. We commenced to be ravenously hungry. No meal satisfied us long. Hunger wakened us when without it we would have slept and dozed out entire days. On the morning of the third day Terry said:

'We have only enough meat for one other meal, Hugh.'

'Fry it for breakfast,' I bade her. 'Oh, I'm stiff and sore.
There's a rock here we must do something about. It gets me
right in the small of the back.'

'But that leaves us nothing for dinner,' she protested.

'I'll get something,' I answered.

'But it's broad daylight.'

'I don't care. I'm too hungry to care.'

I killed a grouse on a hillock right underneath the cave.
Warm as it was we plucked it; Terry stuffed it with oatmeal
and chopped onions and roasted it for four hours on a fire
of turf. In spite of the long cooking the grouse was tough.

'We mustn't let this happen again,' Terry said severely.
'We must pull ourselves together, Hugh. Don't burn the
feathers, boy, they may come in useful.'

We have recalled our reckless carelessness on that day
many times, killing a grouse in broad daylight and cooking
it for a whole afternoon on a smoky fire. We were so hungry
that the world might overlook us and we would not have
heeded.

The chances were all against our being seen, even if
there had been any one in the neighbourhood. We were
absolutely screened from above. The cliff bulging over the
cave, hid most of the gorge as well as our refuge from any
one looking down from its summit. The cave itself lay in a
hollow between two ridges of flat slatey boulders. Thus on
the west, where we made our fire, we could crouch unseen
from every direction except directly opposite on the other
side of the ravine. The sun shone full on that face for most
of the day, lighting it so plainly that we could distinguish the
least movement. It was so precipitous that a man coming into
it would spend most of his time watching his footing, and he
could spare scanty attention for our hillside. Beyond Loch
Coulter the moor extending in a mossy expanse had only
one practicable path which it was easy for us to watch. As
for the smoke of our fire, we purposely heaped on smoky
fuel one evening and went down into the gorge to find how
noticeable it was. The smoke blended so well with the cliff

behind it that we distinguished the one from the other with difficulty though we knew where to look and what we were looking for.

Our next care was to survey our cave. This den, for as yet it deserved no better name, was twenty-two feet long. The opening at the west end was ten feet wide at the base and eight feet high. From the west end to the centre the cave kept these dimensions, but from the centre to the other end it was much smaller. The leaning slab of rock which composed the outer wall had cracked at the centre of its length, probably because of the curve in the cliff and fallen in a little. So the cave bowed inwards from the centre until the east exit was a narrow aperture something over five feet high and three feet wide at the base. Of course, the cave was roughly triangular throughout its length.

Our first problem was to decide which end we should close and which should be our door. The arguments in favour of an entrance at the west end were plausible and numerous. The east opening, being the smaller, would require less work to close it, and a fireplace could easily be built in it. The west entrance would give us plenty of light, whereas if we went to the great labour of closing it we should make the cave almost pitch dark. It was difficult to creep in at the east end without hitting one's head against a jagged edge of rock. And finally, the west end looked forth on high and rugged hills whose soaring peaks were never seen without some exaltation of spirit, whereas the eastern view was drear, grey, flat and immeasurably depressing whenever a cloud went over the sun.

In fact all our wishes were for the west door, with hills and the sunset before us, and it required strong reasons to make us even consider the merits of an east door. They were prosaic merits. Obviously the larger the door the greater the draught it must admit. We dare not let summer cheat us, we must not prefer light to warmth. The prevailing wind in this country was west or south-west. It brought most of the rain; east winds though bitter were dry. Snow storms came from the south. The break in the rock would help to deflect the

weather from the narrow east entrance. We expected that
it would be easy to make a door for the east opening. And
since we meant to build a fireplace in the cave it was wiser
to build it at the broad west end where Terry could move
about freely when she was cooking. Finally, a small entrance
could be camouflaged; it was unlikely to attract attention;
it was only a few paces from the east end of the cave to our
water-pool, a grave consideration in winter. 'The cave will
be dark all the time, Hugh,' Terry said when we came to
a loath decision about the door. 'We should have brought
candles.'

'We'll not be living inside much except for meals and when
we sleep until bad weather comes,' I replied. 'People used
to make candles of sheep's tallow. I wonder would deer-fat
serve the same purpose? Of course we have bog-fir to make
torches but they're smoky and bothersome.'

'We should try for a stag shortly,' she went on. 'I think
it would be a wise idea to salt some venison before we
commence working on the cave. It'll be a nuisance and
a hindrance if we have to interrupt our work and break
up our time hunting for food. Can we salt meat just now,
Hugh? Will it keep?'

'Perfectly,' I assured her.

I was out before daybreak next morning. The wind was
gentle and steady from the west. I put twenty bullets for
the .22 in my pocket, slung the rifle and the binoculars
over my shoulder, made sure my knife had a keen edge,
and left Terry to light a fire while I clambered eastwards
under the cliff, meaning to circumvent the rocks and come
out on the top of the hill above our cave where I was sure
I'd find deer grazing their way back to the forest. I had
not travelled more than a quarter of a mile when I became
aware of half a dozen beasts approaching by the shore of
Loch Coulter. They advanced slowly but steadily, and I
supposed they had been down on the moor all night, eating
the moss crop for which they are so ravenous in spring when
the new horn is growing, and were returning to the hills and
safety for the day. I had dropped immediately I caught sight

of them, and when I made certain they had not seen me I
looked about me for a way of retreat; if they continued their
course they must inevitably wind me and disturb every other
beast within miles. I was lying on a gentle convex slope from
which I could neither go back nor forward. When I turned
my cheek to the west the wind blew gently on it; the deer
were bound to scent me; a grouse made a terrific clamour
beside me, and I cursed its noise and the unlucky chance
which brought the deer.

They still came ahead, delicately skirting the marsh at
the end of the loch. A big yellow-coated stag led them.
He had lost one horn and he carried the other with the
utmost care. When he came amongst the birches above the
loch I could see him sidestepping branches and nursing his
lone horn through the thicket. Light began to dawn more
clearly. Three smaller stags and a hind and a three-quarter-
grown calf followed him. I thought how admirably the calf
would have suited our needs. Again I cursed the grouse
which dinned incessantly; to my astonishment the deer
paid no heed either to the grouse's warning or my wind
which ought by now to have reached them. They climbed
sedately towards me. Now one, now another bent his head
to crop a tempting morsel of grass. The calf lolloped in the
rear, skipping and dancing aside from imaginary obstacles.
I thought he must be in good heart and fat to caper so.
The brutes continued uphill against all the laws of their
kind, straight into my wind. When they were some three
hundred yards distant I loaded the rifle and got out my
glasses and trained them on the birch trees out of which
the calf was emerging. The miracle might continue and
bring them within range. Then the motion of the wind
in the trees told me the reason why the deer kept their
course. The branches could be seen waving uphill, against
the west. I realized I was lying on the edge of dead wind, and
the breeze behind me was met by other currents sweeping
round the hill from the gullies above. When the stags were
a hundred yards beneath me some instinct, or a whiff of
my scent, arrested them. They halted in a bunch round

their leader, all except the calf who came forward with youthful impatience and stared directly at me. He lifted a hind leg and turned his head to lick himself, presenting his neck and shoulders to my view. I aimed carefully at the juncture of his head and neck, for as he stood his heart was a doubtful target, and the neck if properly struck is as fatal as the heart. I heard the bullet strike, and saw him wince. Somehow that moment seemed tremendously important, as if success in this first venture symbolized prosperity for the future. When I saw him run a few yards downhill I knew I had made no mistake. He fell in a heap. His eyes were glazed before I reached him.

He was very small and pathetic, a huddled young creature, dead and slavering blood, and I felt that pain which I can never escape when I have killed a young beast. Nevertheless I wasted no time in bleeding him and gralloching him. As the blood poured out on the ground I regretted that I had not taken a tin or a bowl with me to catch it and carry it home for blood puddings; I consoled myself for that loss by cleaning every vestige of fat from his entrails; I trailed the gralloch to the loch and flung it in for the pike to eat, with the exception of the lower gut which I left inside the beast.

On my way home I climbed up the hill to investigate a stream which cascaded down the rock. I had been afraid that in the heat of summer our little pool would dry up and this discovery reassured me. The water was cold like ice.

'You got a beast,' Terry commented when I arrived at the cave; 'you weren't long. Oh, it's a calf, poor little thing.'

'It will be very tender,' I replied. 'Did you hear anything?'

'Not a sound. Were you far away?'

'Just round the corner. The .22's the weapon for us, quiet and deadly. But when I skin this beast you must make a wrist-strap for me of its skin to carry bullets. You know, a piece of hide about two inches broad to fasten round my wrist with slits cut in it so that I can carry bullets in a handy way. It's a nuisance getting them out of my pocket when

I'm lying down and don't want to make a movement, and the grease gets rubbed off in my pocket, which isn't good for the rifle.'

'Will we salt it right away?' she asked.

'We won't salt it at all,' I answered.

'We *must* salt it. Meat won't keep any time—'

'I found a waterfall along there. The water is as cold as ice. It must rise from a spring higher up. That waterfall will be our larder.'

'But I don't understand, Hugh.'

'If we hang our meat in the fall the cold water will keep it fresh as long as we are likely to leave it. I don't imagine that will be very long. Carrion beasts won't reach it there.'

'I wasn't very happy about salting meat already,' she said.

'We have no fresh vegetables to keep our blood healthy.'

'He's not very fat,' she commented when the skin was off.

'You'll scrub the gut and dry it and stuff it with meal and fat and chopped onions,' I told her.

'Mealy puddings! Oh how lovely. My, don't we live well! If you had kept the bladder and the lungs we could have had haggis, Hugh.'

I tied the carcass with a piece of rope to a stone above the falls so that the water poured all round it. While I was busy about this business Terry stretched the skin on a flat rock, with the inside up, and pegged it out with stones for the sun to dry. We addressed ourselves once more to the problem of making the cave our home.

Not unnaturally we were more timid and anxious than there was any real need, and for some time we could not work more than a few moments without hearing dangerous sounds, or casting scared eyes all around the void scene. When we had eaten we sat down to regiment our time with as much care as if we were hiding in the centre of a populous country. Other people were so near in time, so present in our thoughts, we could not realize that they were far away, and that we were safe; we felt that our escape had been too easy; we had been too lucky; we feared that luck would undo what it had done, and the chance which preserved us might destroy us with equal ease. We made our arrangements against an infinitesimal chance, and accordingly we were hindered at every turn by excess of caution.

We were determined to keep a routine.

'I know what will happen if we don't arrange a time-table,' Terry declared. 'We'll begin like giants, working too much, full of enthusiasm and good intentions. Then we'll get tired of that. We'll overdo the work so much that we'll have to rest. After we rest we won't be so keen on the dirty jobs. We'll dodge them, we'll put them off to a more convenient time. Then we'll commence to grow lazy and untidy. We'll think that this life is only temporary, why should we fret ourselves over things as if they were permanent! We'll say things will do for all the time they're to last—

'Regular hours, proper meals properly cooked—no tea dinners and frying-pan feeds, Hugh!—enough sleep and not too much, our affairs planned ahead, are a prime necessity,' she stated again. 'If one lives by haphazard in civilized surroundings one grows demoralized. It would be fatal here. We have to think about winter. We may not be here but we can't take chances.'

I agreed with her, and for the next few days we conformed to strict rules. We slept out the darkest hours of the night and worked from dawn until nine o'clock. Thereafter I provided firewood for the day and dug the driest turf I could find while Terry cooked a meal. She tidied the cave and washed the dishes with religious care. From ten o'clock we dozed amongst the rocks if the weather was warm. We had dinner at six, and set to work again in the evening. We ate our last meal before daylight left us.

We were forced to change this routine after a couple of nights in which we scarcely slept a wink, so cold and draughty was our cave and so hard our couch.

'We can't carry on like this,' I told Terry. 'We scarcely sleep a wink at night. Once the cave is tight and warm we can sleep in it, but until then we must snatch sleep through the day, or while we can. We daren't risk our health and waste our time lying awake in misery for the sake of a time-table.'

'What can we do at night if we can't sleep?' she asked. 'We can't work, it's too dark—'

We found an occupation for the night-time by going down to the car and stripping it. We brought away its hood and its upholstery, its tools, and its wind-screen; the side-curtains, even the petrol-tank and the sump, and everything that would come loose, brake-rods and controls, torque tubes and stays and number-plates, were all carried to our cave. On our last journey I erased the engine number and every other distinguishing mark with a chisel.

Terry looked at me when I finished the work of destruction.

'That burns our boats,' she murmured.

We had underestimated the labour necessary to build our west wall. Since this gable would hold our fireplace it was necessary to plan it out carefully and build it with extreme care. I had a vague idea in my head for a wall, sloping on the outside from a broad base to a peak at the roof of the cave, in which we would leave a square space for our fireplace and a vertical hole for our chimney. The simplest hearth sufficed to burn peats. To build the wall itself, without a fireplace, would have cost us little difficulty. We had unlimited material to our hands in the heaps of broad flat slabs of stone all around. I am sure we had a sort of fireplace and chimney constructed ten times, only to discover that it was unsteady, or the chimney would not draw when we lit a fire, or the whole top half of the gable collapsed at a touch. We were in despair.

'If we even had round tins, like oil-drums for example,' Terry sighed, 'we could knock the ends out and set them one above the other. We'll be compelled to use our biscuit tins and make a square chimney, Hugh.'

'That will be the very last resort,' I assured her. 'We must keep our stores dry. Surely we aren't going to be beaten at this early date—there must be something—Terry! I have it, drain-pipes!'

I caught her hands and began to dance her round the cave, singing 'Tra la la la la.'

'Let me go, Hugh,' she scolded. 'Drain-pipes would be very nice—if we had drain-pipes.'

'But we have,' I cried, 'they're as good as here. Isn't there a forest at our back-door? Aren't there deer paths in a forest and culverts in deer paths and drain-pipes in culverts?'

We made two night expeditions into Ardverikie Forest with our spade and came back with a couple of drain-pipes each four feet long. Now the masonry went ahead. We selected only those slabs which lay on the surface and were lichen-grown. When we put them in place we kept their weathered edges to the outside, for nothing attracts the eye like a fresh face of rock in country where all else is weathered and moss-grown. The fireplace was a simple thing. We left a vacancy two feet deep and four feet wide in the centre of the inner side of the wall. When we had lined the back and the sides of this space with sheets of metal, once the bodywork of our car, to protect the stone from the heat of our future fire, we brought the wall to a height of three feet. Now we took the most solid slab of rock we could carry and laid it across from side to side above the fireplace to be its lintel. It took us two days to manœuvre a sufficiently large slab into place. Having made it secure we placed one drain-pipe upright at the back of the slab, resting on a cradle of iron rods from the car. We continued our wall round the chimney, upwards to the roof.

The wall was by no means weathertight. A multitude of chinks let in wind from the south and west, especially near the base where our masonry was most inexpert; we had learned as we worked to lay stone upon stone so that each fitted to the other. There were many crannies too under the roof where the wall sloped in and became narrow. Notwithstanding its flaws the wall was solid and its foundations were sure. We were jubilant to have a gable and a chimney. We decided to leave it as it was for a while until we had redded up the interior of the cave. A little draught was pleasant rather than objectionable so long as summer lasted, and we could proof the wall long before winter came.

Terry insisted that we should now make a fireplace.

'We can't work if we aren't properly fed,' she asserted, 'and I can't make decent meals unless I have a fireplace.'

We knew that peats would burn quite well on a flat stone hearth. I had seen Highland houses in which the fireplace was simply a stone dais in the centre of the floor with a hole in the roof above it to let out some of the smoke. We could have built a similar hearth under the chimney with great ease, for it required no more than one or two broad flat stones.

'It would have the advantage that our fire would never go out, even overnight, if we damped it down in the evening. That would save matches,' I told Terry.

Terry was not enthusiastic for a peat-hearth. She argued that such a fire was smoky even in houses with proper chimneys; we could not expect our tiny chimney to draw unless our fire was brisk. Moreover, peats left a very fine ash. If we had a fireplace with a well under the grate the ashes, falling down, were less liable to be sent through the cave by backing winds, and they could be collected and taken out of doors without disturbing the fire or making a mess. She concluded by telling me that she could not possibly cook on a flat hearth. We decided to make a simple fireplace consisting of an iron cradle flanked by two broad stone cheeks upon which pots could simmer and our kindlings dry.

By now we had some skill in our mason-work. Terry picked out stones for me with an eye to their use and place and we were not hindered by the heaps of rejected flags which had gathered round us when we started to make our gable. Hobs and the grate were all we required to build. We raised two cheeks of stone, each a foot wide and as deep as the cavity in the gable, at the sides of the cavity. When these cheeks were six inches high we searched along the shores of Loch Coulter until we found a bank of clay. I spread a good deep layer of the clay over the cheeks and laid six pieces of iron from the car lengthways from cheek to

cheek, embedding their ends in the clay so that they would
make a stable bottom for our grate. As soon as these rods
were in place we added another row of flat stones to the
cheeks. It was easy now to form the front of the grate by
wedging two other lengths of iron above each other under
successive layers of flat stones. We packed every cranny
with clay. To finish the job we wedged one of the car's
number plates flat beneath the top stones of the cheeks so
that it formed a tray on which a kettle could sit. These hobs
were almost a foot high, I twisted a piece of brake-rod to the
shape of the letter S and slipped one bend over a stay which
supported the chimney. While I was making this crook for
our kettle Terry put dead heather and wood into the grate.
I set a match to the heather. She fetched in a kettle of
water and hung it from the crook. We stood with bated
breath while the smoke began to thicken above the grate;
it gathered in the roof of the fireplace; we felt sick for a
moment; if the chimney would not draw our labour and
our zeal were wasted. We could not live in the cave if we
had no fire. The wind was from the east, and we had left the
east entrance to our cave open for the wind to rush through
and aid the chimney. Suddenly the chimney warmed, the
smoke which swirled round our heads was sucked back into
the fireplace, the fire went up in a blaze. We danced, we
gazed at our handiwork, we ran outside to tell each other
to come and see the smoke rising from our chimney. We
made tea and sat in front of the fire, fancying that it was
winter, and the wind howled snow-laden against our gable,
and pans hottered in peace by the side of our own peat fire.

'I wish I had eggs,' Terry sighed. 'I'm sure I could bake
hundreds of fine things on our fire. I could make a cake in
the iron pan, using it for an oven, with a peat smouldering
on the lid.'

'Why do you want eggs?' I asked. 'Can't you bake
without them?'

'Yes,' she agreed doubtfully. 'But how fine it would be
on an *occasion* if we had pancakes, Hugh, with raspberry
jam—'

'Don't tempt me,' I besought her, and interrupted myself to cry, 'We can get eggs!'

'Where's your hen?' Terry mocked.

'We've got better than a hen—gulls—scores of them—in the little loch with the islands beyond Loch Coulter—you know, Loch Glas Choire where we caught bait for the pike.'

'But can we get them?' she asked breathlessly. 'Are the islands easy to reach? When will we go?'

'We can get them easily,' I assured her.

'What a pity we didn't bring waterglass,' she sighed, 'but we aren't really to blame. Who'd have imagined—even if we had lime—'

'What do you want lime for?' I demanded.

'To preserve the eggs, Hugh. You boil salt and quicklime together—'

'But we can get lime, tons of it! Don't you remember the lime-kiln by the roadside at Kinlochlaggan? They burnt lime there forty or fifty years ago. They quarried the lime from an outcrop beside the Pattock. The vein of limestone runs from Loch Laggan to Loch Ericht.'

'Oh, Hugh!'

'The vein is bound to pass near here. We'll find an outcrop somewhere handy, I'm sure of it.'

'If we do find lime we could make mortar for our gable,' she added with rising excitement.

'Yes, and take the hair from deer-skins if we wanted leather,' I continued, as excited as herself.

We went off in the utmost haste to search for limestone. I carried the little rifle with me in case we chanced on game. We found an outcrop of limestone so quickly that I had no opportunity to use the rifle. But on the way home Terry stumbled across a curlew's nest. I tried the eggs in a pool; they sank, and I stowed them in the snout of my cap.

'Must we really take them?' Terry asked with a stricken glance at the nest.

'We can't afford to be squeamish,' I replied. 'We are going to do the same thing to scores of gulls—'

'Gulls are different somehow—'

I burned a lump of limestone in our new grate and boiled the quicklime with an equal quantity of salt. While the brew cooled I hacked out one end of the car's petrol-tank with an axe. We had forgotten a tin-opener.

I hammered down the jagged edges of the tank and washed it and poured in our mixture. Terry put the curlew's eggs in the pickle.

'That's a beginning to our cure,' she said with satisfaction.

'Don't we live well,' Terry said a little later when she had looked at our eggs for the twentieth time. 'How many people in houses live better?'

Our thoughts went out, we could not for long forget that world of houses where men lived, which we had fled to escape.

IT DAWNED ON me suddenly that this is Term day. We ought to pay our rent. I have avoided Terry all morning in case she saw how preoccupied I was, for when she begins to ask me questions I can't hide what I am thinking. It would distress her if I told her that our rent would soon be overdue, and that if it was not paid our belongings would be turned out of the house. I know our landlord and I have little hope that he will be patient. I should have paid our rent for a year in advance. Our exile cannot possibly last more than a year. It would break Terry's heart to think that our house was taken from us, and our stuff flung out to rot in the open, or be stolen by every petty thief in the neighbourhood, and the rooms where we were happy occupied by strangers.

But there may be no house now standing where we lived, no house, no landlord, nothing. How strange it is that I should think of the world we have left as if nothing had happened there; and all the fears which drove us here are so remote that the deepest grief my present mind can accomplish is because I forgot to pay our rent.

But it is not deep grief. It troubles the surface of my mind. If I were really troubled in my heart I could not hide it from her. I have often tried many a time to keep my vexations secret and my unhappiness hid, but she finds them out, and I am glad when I am discovered. These miseries grow light when she knows what they are, and we bear them together. To-day I am vexed, but not deeply, and it is as easy to avoid her as it is difficult to keep my mind on our house and what must become of it because we cannot pay our rent. The house, happy though we were in it, seems remote and trivial. All things seem trivial save the life we live now. We have severed so many bonds, and all have proved so weak, that I scarcely think of our house and our furniture as our own any more save for Terry's sake. If I am vexed it is chiefly because I ought to have remembered to pay our rent. I am equally vexed each time I recall things we should have brought with us. This is strange, that I should be perturbed because I have omitted to do things which would make complete our independence and our severance from our old life; for our present life is no more than a shift, a temporary escape, and all its course, and all our thoughts, should be towards its ending. But it is not so. I am wrapt in the immediate daily events. I have no desires beyond the cave that shelters us and the land that we occupy alone.

We occupy, but it is not occupied, nor ever will be occupied. It lies before me and my eyes that see it, and my feet that walk on it, mark what they see and feel upon my brain, but what they view and what they touch is not changed by them, nor aware of them. We are in the wild land, but not of it; winds and beasts and the brown cladding of moor are of it; to-day and every day they go, they return, and we, who shift and go, have comfort and protection but no home. It is strange that this desolate country, heedless and aloof, should give such comfort and be a sanctuary for the mind.

My head is never so busy as when I am occupied with monotonous work. As I cut peats or walk on the hill a multitude of scarcely related thoughts voice themselves in my brain, and I, like a half-attentive eavesdropper, hear my own mind rehearse the hundred shifts and stratagems, the alternating successes and failures which now elate and again depress us as if it was another's voice I heard telling a half-fabulous story. And all the while I am alert for signs in the country, deer with heads in the air, storm-clouds in the sky, with an attention which seems closer and readier and more instinctive when half of my mind is occupied than when I watch and listen with each sense trained to alertness. I have found myself dropping flat on my face in the heather, and I had to recall my wits from day-dreaming, and reason

and stare before I knew that it was a stag's horn on the
skyline which warned me.

No doubt our continual care to be vigilant has sharpened
my senses and quickened my responses; perhaps a sixth
sense has developed which makes me act automatically; I
feel that the present state of mind I carry with me to the
moss and the hill has deeper roots than a new habit. When
we came here first we were always over-anxious. I strained
my eyes watching for men while I hunted beasts. We were
novices in stealth, too bold and too timorous by uneasy
turns, falling from ecstasy to despair upon a trifle. We
have learned soberness. Our fears and our self-satisfaction
cannot now overthrow each other in the twinkling of an
eye, nor make our life a din of contending emotions. We
take each moment's task at its momentary value. We are
not ready to feel that the entire future hangs on the balance
of the precarious present.

I find myself becoming more matter of fact every day.
When I rehearse the tale of recent weeks, as I go to stalk
in the forest, it is the events of these weeks I remember,
seldom the feelings that accompanied them, though I am
aware that when the events occurred our joy and pride in
them, if they were successful, our misery, if they betrayed
us, seemed to fill the world.

I think I am growing contented. I have been struggling
against contentment for many days. I scourged myself,
saying our plight was desperate; the hands of all men
were against us; the future had no light; we lived on
the edge of a world gone mad; our house was forfeit and
we were in truth homeless outcasts. The world was at war.

I strove in vain to foster discontent. No sooner had I begun
working in the peat-moss than my labour there used all my
strength, and my head refused to vex itself with future woes
or other men's grief.

We cut our peats from a deep bank of moss which lies in
a pocket of rock on the hill-top above our cave. The wind
is sweet on that high eminence. It comes from the sea.

If we take things more casually now, it is not because

difficulties have vanished or diminished. We have hard problems to solve every day. Some difficulties increase. Though I have become a better stalker, though I have studied the morning mist in the corries until I know almost every wind that blows, though I go after deer without the exaggerated caution which used to defeat me more often than it aided me, stalking is no mere mechanical occupation like a visit to a killing-house to slaughter a sheep. I have spent many long days on the hill since April passed and come home empty. During April I did not go far afield for meat. I went out at dawn and hid to leeward of some gully through which the deer passed on their return from the moss-crop. In a very short time the deer grew scary, and it dawned on us that we were very short-sighted. We had already frightened the neighbourhood by our mere presence; if we continued to kill beasts within a mile or two of the cave they would forsake the locality.

'I'll have to go farther out,' I told Terry. 'Grouse are so wild already they get up half a mile before I come near them, and as for deer they watch us from the skyline and bolt at our least movement. We'll make this bit of ground a sanctuary, and never kill inside it unless there's dire need. We may not want to go far out for our meat when winter comes.'

'Must you go a great distance?' Terry asked anxiously.

'Farther every day I'm afraid. As summer comes on and the flies arrive the deer will move right up to the summits—you mustn't worry, honey. I'll be quite safe.'

Often and often I come home without meat, tired, wet, and dispirited. Variable winds, an alert beast in another quarter altogether from those I am stalking, flat slopes where I creep and crawl in vain efforts to come within shooting distance of a herd, my own haste or breathlessness, make stalking a gamble and give it zest too. There is a great deal of satisfaction in dropping a nobber with the .22 at a hundred yards range. I feel less like a butcher after a difficult stalk. Of course when I see deer a couple of hundred yards away that I can in nowise approach I long for the .303. The little rifle is deadly enough if it is held straight at distances up

to a hundred yards. Beyond that hitting and killing with
it is a risk which I do not often take; I have no wish to
wound beasts or merely frighten them, and many a time I
have spent two hours grovelling in a slimy bog to discover
that it was useless going farther. Then I turn my back on
the herd I am stalking; they graze in peace while I snake
back the way I had come.

Tired and vexed and footsore though I may be, I never
draw near the place we have made our home without a
feeling like ecstasy flooding over me. The surge of rock
out of the great gorge, the loud wind amongst the gullies in
that cliffy hill which overhang our cave, the blind expanse
of the vacant world, spring's colours in the sky and on the
moor, change all my spirits.

Terry has hot water and dry clothes waiting for me at
whatever time I come home. When I am cheerful, with half
a young deer over my shoulder and the forequarters hidden
safely on the hill, I step gently to take her by surprise. I
never can use enough stealth for that though I would swear
my footfall falls no louder than rain, or the hunting fox's
pad, amongst the rocks. She is out of the cave to greet
me and while I hand her the rifle to wipe dry and the
telescope to clean she bubbles over with questions, praise
for my success, news of her own doings through the day.
If the weather is warm we carry my change of clothes to
the waterfall and I strip to bathe under its icy flood; she
rinses out my dirty stockings as I dry myself. When I am
out the livelong day (for if I get nothing between dawn
and the strength of morning I hole up wherever day finds
me, waiting for evening) I can never bear to rest in the
cave. I choke for breath inside. Like one whose appetite is
whetted by what it feeds on I grudge each moment of the day
that passes without my seeing the open country. I remember
one evening when we skinned a fat yeld hind. Terry made
supper. I sat at the mouth of the cave, and evening grew
to night beneath my gaze; the shadowed sun went down
into its western sea beyond the hills and every valley was
darkened until the mazy woods were one with the general

dusk. Away to the north the Olympic peak of Craig Dhu glowed in azure light above its harboured straths. I heard Terry come out beside me.

'I'd have died in prison, Terry,' I said.

'We have done for ourselves, finished ourselves, given ourselves up bound and captive,' she whispered. 'Never to escape, Hugh.'

'Escape!' I said, surprised by her tone, and turned to look at her. Her face was pale, her eyes, fixed on the islanded hills, seemed to grow large and take in the light which still shone over these proud peaks. Her face was like that of one transfigured.

She spread her hands over the gorge, the moor, and all our country under the dappled sky.

'When we grafted ourselves to this wild stock,' she said in a low voice.

'Here's no grafting,' I told her sadly. 'We're bound to it, as if we were made of it, but what binds it to us?' I made a puff of breath with my lips. 'A little breath, some dust—and this place as if we never were.'

She shook her head.

'A little dust makes it and us one,' she said. 'You must be dying with hunger, Hugh.'

'I'm past being hungry,' I confessed. 'I could have eaten heather two hours ago.'

'Had you a difficult time?' she inquired. I told her about my adventures round the Durc where the eagles nest, and I saw a wren hopping from boulder to boulder under the shadow of its great neighbours' wings. I halted my recital to ask, half-jesting, 'What grows on our wild stock, Terry, wild roses or a crown of thorns?'

'Many a crown of thorns on men's brows this day,' she murmured. 'I wonder what's happening in the world?'

Dangers as well as empty days accompany my stalking. I had so many living enemies to look for, wary deer and chance strangers from the world of men, that I grew careless about the natural dangers of the country. In the beginning of May I went off before dawn as usual to go into Ardverikie

Forest. There had been frost, and white rime lightened the gloom and let me pick my way amongst the hags into which I generally floundered on these morning excursions. It was essential to get meat; our last piece of boiled venison was in my pocket. We had let ourselves run short while we delved our peats and set them up to dry. Since we depended on meat a great deal, and saved our stores as far as possible, we required to kill something very frequently. We had enjoyed voracious appetites since we arrived at the cave. So far I had brought home mostly calves and nobbers, but the stags were putting on flesh after their winter hunger, and this day I set my mind on a grown beast.

The wind was erratic and an unlucky breath from the south spoiled my first stalk. It had been a long difficult business. I was compelled to work uphill towards the herd I picked out on the ridge of Meall nan Eacan. The stags were lying as usual with their heads downhill so that most of my progress up the concave ascent was on my belly. The day was well advanced before I got near my quarry. When they winded me it was too late to begin a fresh stalk. I crouched in heather to sleep out the middle of the day.

When the sun began to near the west I scanned the shoulder of the Farrow, about three miles away in a direct line, but five or six miles distant by the route I must follow, over the hill on which I hid, down a steep corrie, across the Sluie valley, and up the Farrow itself. If I could cross the glen without being observed it would be easy to approach my deer. I hurried on my way, trusting to the shadow of night which already filled the valley to hide me. When I came into the floor of the valley my work began. Hundreds of deer had appeared on the slope of the Farrow; they were moving slowly downhill towards the moors where they would feed all night, but I could not reckon on their arriving near me before it grew too dark to shoot. I advanced by inches over the flat in full view of any deer that chanced to look my way. I could not even risk to jump the Sluie stream which flowed across my path. I soaked myself to the skin creeping through a pool on my hands and knees, with the water round my shoulders. Eventually I came under the curve of the hill and lay a moment to rest. The climb before me was steep and the light was rapidly degenerating. I made what haste I could towards the herd I marked. When I reached the place where I saw them they were no longer there. I sat down in despair. As I looked idly across the lip of the Durc I saw a hind's head on the far side with the eyes gazing directly at me. My first shot missed completely. I was too excited and shaken to aim straight. The second broke her shoulder. She tried to turn on the narrow ledge where she was standing. She tumbled as she put her weight on the useless leg; another shot took her in the chest and she sprang clear from her ledge, over the sheer rock, into the depths of the ravine. I could hear her body striking successive ledges and a small avalanche of stones accompanied her. Without pausing to think if the way down was practicable I rushed over the edge of the gorge and began to lower myself from boulder to boulder so that I could see where she had fallen and make sure that she was dead.

I glimpsed her, as it seemed vertically beneath me, striving to rise to her feet. She was half covered with stones and shingle. I could not see to shoot her in the heart. Again I let myself down, zigzagging round vertical rocks and lying on my belly across boulders which I could not circumvent, slithering and bracing myself down gravel-slides. The hind, when I saw her next, seemed motionless. I should have known the fall would kill her even if my bullets failed, but I was too excited for such calm thoughts as would have restrained me from descending the side of the Durc at its steepest part. I was carrying my rifle in my hand. I now slung it across my shoulder and continued my descent with my heart in my mouth at each step, for my frenzied excitement had spent itself and the height above me seemed unscalable; the fall beneath was sheer, and I crouched between heaven and earth on the brink of a precipice. When I was only thirty feet above the hind, but still a good deal higher from the floor of the cañon—for she had been checked in her fall by boulders—I reached a descent which I could not

escape by going round it; nor could I go back; I could
scarcely believe that I had come from that overhanging lip
I saw above me, black against the sky. I drew back in panic
from the verge of the cliff with my feet on a ledge which
seemed more inadequate and slippery every moment. At
first I stood there with my hands idle. Soon I grew dizzy
and clutched tufts of heather to keep myself from falling.
All at once I saw the hind make a desperate effort. She
flung herself clear of the stones which lay on her. It was
her death-struggle but that idea never entered my head. I
grew excited again and dragged the rifle from my shoulder.
As I got it free my feet slipped. I felt myself plunging over
the abyss. I saw the hind sinking on her side; then I struck
the ground; instead of the horrid jarring of broken bones I
felt an equally horrible soft squelching shock. Before I could
gather my wits or realize where I had fallen I was waist deep
in a green bog beside the stream which drains the Durc. The
rifle flew out of my grasp and lodged between two boulders
close to the burn.

If it had gone beyond my reach I should have drowned in
that filthy stinking hole without much delay. I shall never
forget the foul smell of the morass. Green bubbles burst in
the scum around me. My strongest feeling as I sank was not
fear but revulsion; to choke submerged in this abominable
stew!—I strained to reach the rifle and succeeded in
clasping the tips of the fingers of my left hand round the
barrel. When I put my weight on the barrel it did not move.
It was wedged securely; now I could breathe, and now feel
fear; I pulled and struggled to escape. The bog clung to me.

I had not enough strength in my fingers to pull myself
nearer to the side. I had indeed scarcely enough strength
to keep myself from sinking farther, and already my fingers
were losing their grip, growing numb, slipping from the
smooth steel. I set my teeth and made myself quit labouring
and struggling so that I could think, before it was too late. I
saw a dreadful picture of myself hanging there until my left
hand released its hold, and I went down.

A mood of apathy came over me. Rest was sweet, to close

one's eyes; a violent desire for life followed immediately afterwards. I thought of a hundred expedients. No doubt there were only seconds between my falling into the bog and the moment when I dragged the leather belt from my waist with my right hand; it was all I could do to force myself to thrust my hand into the slime to unloosen my belt. I was wearing a broad leather belt, stiff enough to push forward with my right hand until it passed underneath the barrel of the rifle. I got the tip of the forefinger of my left hand round the edge of the belt. With bated breath I worked the belt between my other fingers. Then I had both ends in my hand, in my two hands; I lay with closed eyes, resting my weight on the line that held my life. I had to wait until strength returned to my left hand before I could drag myself free. I was free; I lay on my face on the ground with my hands gripping the solid dear earth. I was sick and spent, but the beast which cost so much must be brought home. I gralloched the hind and severed her backbone. When the forequarters were happed with stones to keep them safe from carrion beasts and birds I got the hindquarters over my head, with a haunch on each side of my neck and the legs in my hands. Staggering, tripping, reeling, I blundered home.

Terry was distracted with anxiety, and I could not clean all the mire from my clothes. I concocted a story which sounded false as I told it. Oh, how sweet it was to be clean, to lie down, to sleep!

We have had adventures, but for the most part our life is simple, laborious, and quiet. We had a great deal of work that we knew we must do. Each task as we accomplished it led to others that we had not thought of. As soon as our gable was erected we went into the cave to plan what we must do in it. The floor was very uneven; the bare rock protruded through the thin layer of peaty ground. We chipped away as much of these outcrops as we could. Of course the floor of the cave, being part of the hill-side, had a considerable list as well as inequalities, though fortunately it sloped less steeply than the ground outside. A few inches

of fall made matters very uncomfortable for us, especially
when the gable was built and shut out most of our light.
We had to sleep across the floor with our feet downhill, and
if we moved we were liable to roll to the bottom side of the
cave, amongst the pots and tins and duffle. If we wakened
suddenly and lifted our heads we were sure to strike them
on the rock.

Until the last stone was laid in the gable the cave was well
lighted. We could see where we were putting our feet. But
immediately the wall had shut out the sun the cave grew
pitch dark. We must have light to illumine our work. We
laboured for a week by the smoky flare of a bog-fir torch and
the glimmer of our fire. If we made a fire big enough to light
the cave it was too hot for working. Our torches produced
more smoke than illumination. To crown our misfortunes
the wind, which had been blowing gently from the south-east
since we kindled our first fire in the new grate, commenced
to back, and after several shifts it finally fetched up in the
south-west.

I suppose we were foolish to imagine that because our
chimney drew at its first trial it would never smoke, whatever
the wind. No sooner had the breeze gone to the west of south
than smoke started to belch into the cave, intermittently at
first, and afterwards, when the wind went near west, almost
as if the cave had become the chimney.

We are not very expert yet in this life, but I am afraid that
we were absolute fools then. We fell into the utmost anguish
at this reverse. I was all for knocking down the gable we had
built so painfully and letting the weather do its worst. Terry
cried, I could have cried too if I had not flown into a rage
and kicked the fireplace with all my strength, loosening the
bars we had spent days fixing.

Our eyes smarted, our nerves were on edge, we squabbled
like nervous children, going into a rage without provocation
and becoming abjectly penitent the next moment. We set
ourselves to filling the chinks in our wall, but we had neither
enthusiasm nor interest in our work.

'Will we make lime and mix mortar?' Terry asked.

'How long do you think we've got to patch this filthy wall?' I demanded. 'Years?'

'You don't need to snap my head off,' she retorted.

We brought clay in a pail from the lochside and plastered the crevices. As we had sunk to immeasurable depths on a reverse, so a little success elated us. When the wall was proofed and lapped in clay our fire blazed up, the cave cleared of smoke, we looked at each other with radiant pride, forgetting every squabble in the moment of accomplishment.

The cure was not quite complete. Occasionally a gust drove smoke down the chimney, though it was no worse in that respect than many chimneys in houses we had seen. But I was encouraged by our victory and determined to make it final. At nightfall one day I took the second drain-pipe we had brought from Ardverikie and up-ended it over our chimney-can. When it was in place and fixed with a few stays I heard Terry's voice crying from inside the cave. I rushed to find out what had happened.

'Look, Hugh!' she exclaimed, pointing to the fire. It blazed merrily and the air of the cave was sweet and clean.

'We've done it, we've done it!' I shouted, and hastened to placate fate by adding: 'Of course the trouble is that we must take the pipe down through the day in case it's noticed.'

'I don't care if it comes down twice an hour,' Terry said in an enraptured voice. 'Now we can get ahead with our house. What about light, Hugh? We won't let a trifle like light prevent us now.'

'I could kill a sheep,' I said slowly, 'and make candles of the tallow.'

Terry shook her head.

'We're not going to become sheep-stealers for the sake of a candle,' she returned.

I laughed at her reproof.

'Oh, I didn't intend to take a sheep from a farm,' I returned; 'but to stalk one of the brutes that are running wild in the forest and warning deer whenever I come in sight—if I *could* stalk them! They're wilder than deer and they whistle when they see you, standing on the top of every craggy knoll to give warning! Maybe you're right. Don't you fancy a nice mutton chop? They'd be as tough as leather and as thin as rakes probably.'

The deer I had killed as yet were very lean, with scarcely any fat on their guts, and we required what little there was for cooking; if there was any to spare Terry salted it against the future. In the commencement of May we happened to recollect that our fishing-tackle had never been looked at. I caught a fry of small trout on Loch Coulter, and put out set lines for pike. When we returned to inspect our lines we had two pike weighing eight or nine pounds each. I opened them by the loch-side to rebait my hooks with their entrails. They were full of soft oily fat. I carried it to the cave in triumph. We melted out the oil in a pan and added the scum of fat which rose to the surface of the water in which we boiled our pike. We were left with a good pint of oil.

I drained a milk-tin by cutting two holes in one end and blowing through one hole while the milk ran out of the other. Terry swilled out the residue of milk with boiling water and I went to the lochside for strong stalks of green rushes. I peeled the skin away from the pith of the rushes and laid the short lengths of pith to dry before our fire. Terry half-filled the tin with oil. Next we soaked two lengths of pith in oil and stuck them through the holes in the tin so that their bottom ends were in the oil and each protruded about an inch from the tin. We put a light to our wicks. They burned with a tiny yellow spluttering flame. With the light of our fire besides we had sufficient illumination for our work, and if we required more light we could bore other holes in the tin and add extra wicks.

'Can we always get pike?' Terry asked anxiously, 'or must we catch as many as possible just now and extract enough oil for winter?'

'They ought to be still fatter in winter,' I answered. 'But it would be a wise plan to gather a store of oil just now in case the weather is too wild later on. The loch will freeze over,' I went on.

'Then if we can get oil at any time I'm going to make dubbin for our shoes,' she said.

We had forgotten to bring boot polish with us. We had been using the offal which remained when Terry melted out the deer fat to smear our shoes. It kept them soft and waterproof for a time, but it quickly wore off. My boots had begun to bleach and show signs of wear at the toes. The rank heather and stones through which I had to go on my way to the forest were hard on boots. Terry collected soot from the chimney and mixed it to a stiff paste with some pike oil. The mixture proved very successful. It seemed to feed the leather and give it a gloss as well as waterproof it.

When I saw Terry busy making her dubbin I thought I had better do something to protect the toes of my boots. We had a few knots of limestone remaining from what we brought home to make the pickle for our eggs and I burnt them and made a stiff paste of the quicklime with water. This paste I spread over the outside of a square of deer skin. In a few days I washed away the lime and all the hair came with it. I laid the bare skin on a rock with stones at the corners to keep it taut and treated it liberally with the dubbin. Then I cut two strips an inch wide and three inches long and nailed them with brass rivets, of which we had a half-pound, round the toes of my boots. Terry meanwhile cut two other pieces from our deer-leather to make anklets for me. They were long enough to encircle my legs over the tops of my boots, and three inches broad. She sewed a long thin strip of leather to one end of each anklet which would go twice round my legs and hold the anklets in place like the tapes of puttees. These fastenings were only temporary. As soon as we could spare more time she intended to steal the back-straps from two pairs of my breeches and use their buckles for my anklets.

For the moment, after I had admired my boots and anklets, we determined to abjure the hundreds of tempting refinements which were constantly suggesting themselves, and to devote all our attention to making the cave comfortable. Fortunately the ground of the floor was slightly deeper under the cliff than on the outer side of the cave, and we rectified the floor's list by digging a few inches from the top side and spreading out the earth lower down. We finally produced a fairly flat smooth surface, though it was still soft. We pounded the floor with flat heavy stones until it was so hard that my tackety boots made no impression in it though I jumped and danced.

From our first arrival in the cave we were inconvenienced by lack of a place in which to stow our belongings. We struggled along while the west end was open and the cave was light. Thereafter we could no longer carry bulky obstacles out of doors when they were in the way. We were always tripping over bedding, clothes, pots and tools, and besides our annoyance we had a permanent fear in case we broke something irreplaceable. We could only get ahead with our work because Terry did little except stay beside me moving things from one place to another as I digged or pounded, and that of course meant that our work went at the rate of one pair of hands instead of two.

We realized that we could never make progress until we had a place in which to stow our furniture. Even in tins our food became damp, and our bedding required to be aired every day. Our health as well as our comfort demanded cupboards.

'We ought to have left two openings in the wall beside the fireplace for pots and dishes,' I said. But the wall would have been too weak had we done that.

'Could we not make holes in the rock and drive pegs into them,' Terry suggested.

We tried and failed to drive a hole in the rock.

'In fact we're beat,' Terry said in a melancholy voice. 'Och then I suppose we can't do anything but struggle away as best we can. Oh I do hate to see this litter on the floor, everything spoiling—'

While we were tormenting our heads for a solution to this problem another presented itself. We were most uncomfortable sleeping on the floor, even after the floor was levelled. We had only enough bedclothes to keep us warm and of course we could not spare to lay any underneath us in place of a mattress to relieve the hardness of the floor. To make matters worse it was necessary to roll up our bed whenever we wakened since we needed all the cave's space to cook and work in. This second objection to our bed on the floor hindered us from making a heather couch. We knew that a properly made heather-bed was softer than the softest bed of down. You gather young heather and pack it upright in a square frame until the whole frame is tightly filled. We could have made a simpler bed of heather or bracken heaped on the floor. The bracken or heather would scatter through the cave. It would become damp. It could not be replaced by dry heather in winter.

Furthermore every bed we envisaged on the floor would expose us to the draught which blew towards the fireplace.

'If we had a hammock—' Terry lamented after a long futile discussion.

'Terry! Terry!' I cried in rapture. 'Oh, what a fool I am not to have thought of it—'

'Thought of what?' she asked curiously, regarding my joyful antics without enthusiasm. 'Do you mean a hammock, Hugh? Where could we sling it? Wouldn't it be in our way equally with a bed on the floor?'

I refused to tell her what my plan was, though she implored me to divulge it.

'It mightn't be a success,' I put her off. Of course, if I had not been fairly certain of its success I should have let her into the secret, and avoided the danger of solitary discomfiture.

Leaving her to work in the cave, I went to the birch wood beside Loch Coulter with the heavy axe and cut down and trimmed six good straight young birch trees. When I had fetched them to the cave I took measurements of the distances from the outer edge of the floor and from the inner edge to the peak of the roof; I took these measurements inside the cave close by the fireplace, four feet from the fireplace, and ten feet from the fireplace. I cut the poles, one for each measurement, but every pole three inches or thereby longer than the measurement, and I made holes in the floor at the places where I had taken the measurements. I now carried the poles into the cave and set them up in the places I had measured for them, with their butt ends in the holes in the floor and their points just crossing underneath the roof. I lashed each pair together where they crossed so that I had as it were three pairs of rafters. As soon as this was done I returned to the wood and found a slender birch tree from which I cut a straight ten-foot length. I searched again for rowan saplings about two inches thick; I collected six of these and they were likewise ten feet long.

When these in turn were brought to the cave I packed the holes in the floor with small stones and tamped the stones with clay and pounded it until the rafters were as firm at the base as I could make them. Thereafter I slipped the ten-foot birch along the roof until the end touched the chimney-wall. It rested safely in the crutch of the three crossed rafters, and I lashed it there. The rowan saplings were likewise tied to the rafters at equal distances down the sides of the cave; I had a framework ready for my plan.

Terry watched me with an expression half-curious, half-rebellious, on her face.

'It's not fair, Hugh,' she cried out at length, 'you ought to tell me what you are doing. Anyway,' she concluded illogically, 'I don't believe you know yourself, unless you think the roof is about to fall, and how am I to cook with that cat's cradle dangling over my head?'

Without saying a word I took a pan and pushed its handle between the lowest cross-piece of my framework and the rock, on the down side of the cave.

'A rack!' cried Terry, clapping her hands and hastening to arrange the other pots alongside the first.

'Is that what you meant?' she asked anxiously.

'Partly,' I replied, laughing at her eagerness.

'What's next?' she wanted to know.

'We're going for a walk,' I told her. Her face clouded again.

'Don't tease me, Hugh,' she exclaimed. 'You're very bad to me.'

'Since we haven't any nails of our own we must steal some,' I hastened to explain, 'so we'll walk as far west as the Ardverikie march and get a few staples from the deer-fence.'

'Isn't that very wrong of us?' she asked. 'What are we going to do with staples?'

'Sling our hammock, Terry.'

'From this frame, Hugh?' she asked in dubious tones. 'Oh—I see. But won't it be in our way?'

I explained that the hammock would be attached permanently on one side, but on the other it would be fixed in such a way that we could disengage it from the frame and swing it upwards flat against the wall when it was out of use.

'Like a wall-bed in a flat!' she cried, all enthusiasm. 'My! it was clever of you to think that out, Hugh. Can we go for the staples at once? I'm dying to see—isn't it exciting? What fun we're having, you and I together.'

We fetched four posts which happened to be slack and might come in useful as well as a pocketful of staples from the Ardverikie fence. Terry now insisted that she must be allowed to share in the job, so while I built a rectangular frame four feet wide and six feet long with stout rowan saplings she stripped the hood of our car from its stays and ribs. She cut a piece of the hood to the shape of the hammock-frame but a few inches wider to allow the material to be turned round the side-pieces and end-pieces of the frame when it was ready for sewing. As soon as we had stretched the canvas taut Terry sewed it in place. I drove staples into the four rafters farthest from the fire, and into the middle cross-pieces between these rafters.

We fetched several yards of wire from the fence in Ardverikie Forest and cut it into lengths of a foot. I looped eight of these pieces of wire through the staples on the up side of the cave, and, passing the ends of the wires round one side of the hammock, twisted them until they were safe from coming loose, and all were of the same length. Thereafter I bent eight other wires to the shape of the sneck of a farm gate. The loop ends encircled the opposite side of the hammock-frame from that I had already fixed while the right-angled ends engaged with staples in the rafters and cross-pieces on the lower side of the cave. A few staples hammered into the roof beam held the hammock against the wall while it was tilted up and not in use. We regarded our work in silence.

'We'll be above the draught to the chimney too!' Terry exclaimed. 'What are we going to do next, Hugh?'

It was darkling and I was tired with walking and working. 'Enjoy the first night's comfortable sleep we've had since we came here,' I told her.

'We need a mantelpiece—we need chairs and a table—oh, thousands of things,' she said. 'I'm sleepy too. Let down the hammock, boy. I'm tired to death, oh so sleepy. Clever, clever Hugh.'

WHEN I WAKENED this morning I half expected to see fresh snow on the tops. I think I should have been glad of snow, anything to break the monotony of this rain-swept week. The day was cold enough for winter.

'Still raining, Hugh?' Terry asked from amongst the blankets.

'Oh get up and see for yourself,' I answered in a rage.

'Still raining then,' she told herself with a sigh. 'Still pelting rain.'

'I wouldn't care if it did pelt,' I went on savagely. 'It's this cold drizzle that gets on my nerves.'

'Are you coming back to bed?' she inquired.,

'What's the use of that?' I demanded. 'What's the use of anything. Damn these kindlings, won't they ever catch! There's not a dry peat nor a dry stick—I'm fed up! fed up! fed up!'

'Poor boy,' she murmured.

'Don't "Poor boy!" me!' I raged. 'Get up and see if you can make this fire burn. How do you expect me to move with that filthy hammock right across the place?'

She sat up and gazed at me with round sleepy eyes, and passed her hand abstractedly through her hair.

'Are you in a rage with me, Hugh?' she asked.

'No I'm not,' I retorted. 'Why should I be in a rage with you?—I don't know what I am—oh, can't you leave me alone and not bother me?'

I got down on my knees before the fire to puff and blow into its black sodden heart. For all my breath and all the ashes that blew out into my face the sticks would not take.

Terry began to put on her clothes with the most sober expression.

'Let me do it,' she said, gently pushing me aside. I stood up to watch her. She whittled slivers of fir from a root and laid them in the fireplace and poured a little pike-oil on them. In a moment a tongue of flame came licking up, and as it grew she added splinters of wood until it was bright and strong. I bent down beside her to heap on roots. When the wet skin of the sticks dried they caught fire suddenly, and went up in a blaze which filled the chimney and lighted the cave to its farthest corner.

'Now, Hugh,' she said.

'I'm sorry I was cross—' I began in conscience-stricken tones; 'you mustn't pay any attention to me.'

'But really, Hugh,' she expostulated, 'you can scarcely expect me to ignore you when you make such a loud noise.'

'Was I making an awful noise?' I murmured.

'You're very violent, my dear,' she continued.

'You mustn't heed me—' I began, and hesitated. 'I was going to give you a cup of tea in bed,' I said discontentedly.

'Run and look at the weather and then we'll have a cup by the fire instead,' she encouraged me.

I went slowly to the door.

'Terry!' I cried when I looked outside. 'Terry, the sun!'

She came running, half-clad as she was, to view the break in the mist through which the effulgent sun showed momentarily. We gazed at each other and laughed with delight and going outside we capered crazily amongst wet heather and slippery rocks until we were breathless. The cave and a few yards around lay in a pool of sunlight, but everywhere else there was thick mist. Our narrow corner, islanded in mist and that strange silence of a misty day, grew warm. Though many burns made a sound the world was silent.

'We'll have our breakfast outside,' I declared. 'As sure as death I thought the sun was gone away for good and all. Harken, did you hear a grouse?'

'Och, leave it in peace,' she said, arresting me with her

hand. 'We don't need meat at the moment, Hugh. I wouldn't like to shoot it—it's like an envoy—a harbinger—'

'Of better days?'

'And better temper.'

'Oh, it was the drizzle that got on my nerves!' I said. 'If rain comes down properly I like it. It's fine to see the burns get up and hear them roar; I love to stand at the door watching the spates come over the rocks as white as snow. Something's happening when it comes a flood and the wilder it is the surer you know that it's got to end some time. If you stay inside how warm and dry and comfortable you are, and if you go out, then you get soaked and that's all. But this drizzle, this mist, this clamminess that's neither wet nor dry nor properly cold nor warm, it's not enough to make you bide indoors, and when you go out it seeps and creeps until you're wet and cold and miserable to the very marrow of your bones. You can't see, you can't think—I like wild weather—'

'Yes,' was all she said.

'It's terrible to let a little mist get the better of me,' I went on ruefully.

'We are very close to the weather here, Hugh,' she said.

'Imagine it, we were pleased to see the rain—' I began.

'I'm quite pleased it came,' she interrupted. 'It taught us lessons we were sadly needing.'

'I suppose it did,' I assented grudgingly, and then, suspicious of her meaning, I demanded, 'What did it teach us, Terry?'

'You know quite well,' she returned. 'The only way we learn things, Hugh, is by feeling them, suffering them. If we had all good weather and every day sunny until winter arrived we'd never discover how to keep our clothes dry, or make use of a fine interval—or avoid knocking against each other.'

'A damned expensive way of learning,' I grumbled. 'My peats will be as wet as muck.'

'Didn't you make them into heaps?'

'Yes, but that wouldn't save them.'

'You can't tell until you've seen them. What's the use of meeting trouble, Hugh? If they're wet they'll dry. We can cut more. A few hot days will cure all the harm that's been done. But if we had no bad weather till winter, we'd see our stuff being spoilt then, without any hope of heat and sun to mend it.

'And our cave is really fit for living in,' she added.

When the hammock was erected we made a mantel-shelf over the fireplace by laying six rowan saplings side by side from one wall of the cave to the other. They made a fairly level shelf and I was pleased with it but Terry did not rest content until she sewed the relics of our car hood into a narrow strip long enough to cover the shelf. She went out furtively leaving me to arrange our teapot, my watch, the tin which served for a tea-caddy, and a variety of other small things on the mantelpiece. She returned in a few minutes with her arms full of bell-heather, rowan-blossom, a few sprays from a gean tree that we found growing in a sheltered corner by Loch Coulter, and crow-foot, buttercups, and wild clover from a grassy plot that had once been occupied by a house of which the ruins were still visible. Probably it had been a summer-shieling. We were very fond of that plot of green. We often wondered about the people who had lived there. Terry filled milk-tins with water to hold her flowers and arranged her vases on the shelf.

'You should have fetched some nettles too,' I said, half-mocking.

'That's cruel of you, Hugh,' she said in a hurt voice.

'We could eat them. People used them for a vegetable in the last war.' We admired each other's work for a little while. Then I made loops of wire to hang from the rafters and hold the rifles and our tools. While Terry was stowing away our tins of food on the wall-ends of the mantelshelf, and suspending dishes and pans and clothes from the rafters, I sawed the four posts we had taken from Ardverikie to equal lengths of a little less than three feet. Using these posts for legs and the straightest branches I could find for ends and sides I constructed the rough skeleton of a table. We were

at a loss for a top to our table. I suggested a deer skin, but
Terry doubted whether our curing was effective enough for
such an important purpose. Eventually we found a broad
thin slab of rock which I trimmed roughly and laid on the
framework. Our table was ready.

Chairs were our next thought. We had the cushions from
the car, two front cushions and a long seat from the back.
They were comfortable but if they were laid on the ground
they were much too low. When I proposed to make stools
of turves Terry pointed out that they would make the place
dirty and they could not be moved from place to place.
I agreed very reluctantly, and in the end we contrived
serviceable though shaky stools from birch saplings.

Our cave was gradually assuming the appearance of a
dwelling. With a good fire burning and the milk-tin lamp
shedding its light from the mantelshelf, it was both gay and
snug. The floor was strewn with deer-skins; we sat down
a hundred times a day, on our own chairs by the fire, to
regard our achievements. When the door was closed with
deer-skin curtains no draught entered, whatever the wind's
direction. The small wood violets that Terry gathered every
day, even when rain fell and mist covered the land, made a
faint perfume.

All the while we were busy with these improvements the
rain kept falling, and mist drew closer every day. At first I
was pleased with the weather. I had work indoors to occupy
me. The wind and the rain came up so thunderously out
of the west, the waters rose with such wild haste, I was
exhilarated, I kept running from admiring the cave, which
did not let in a drop of water, to the doorway whence I
could watch the storm sweep down the gorge beneath me.
Our little trickle of a stream was now a cascade that sprayed
us with mist when we went near to fetch water. I loved to
stand beside the loud fall, and when I was wet to strip my
clothes from me and dry them in front of our fire.

I had made a basin of clay to catch the runnel of our
stream and make it easy to lift water even in dry weather.
It survived the first violent flood. The burn came down so

full that it overleaped the trough to fall in gouts and thunder
yards away from the foot of the cliff. Then the rain abated,
yielding to a steady drizzle, and the burn went down; its
force came directly on my cistern and washed it away in a
few moments. I had no more work to do indoors. Terry was
busy cooking, and cleaning and drying wet clothes. I was
idle and miserable. When I ventured out to view my peats
or to fetch in firewood my clothes were wetted but never
soaked. They had to be taken off and dried as if they were
thoroughly wet. The cave was perpetually festooned with my
steaming clothes; their smell pervaded the place; we could
not move without brushing our faces against dank cloth.

I was full of ambitious plans for a day or two.

'We could easily make a water-wheel with one of the
back-wheels of the car,' I told Terry, 'couple it up to the
dynamo, and give ourselves electric light.'

'We could do that later,' she said in her most matter-of-fact
voice. 'Do you mind running out with this basin of dirty
water?'

She was very careful that we should always throw out our
slops a long way from the cave. I was tempted to fling down
the dishwater at the very door of the cave but I was in the
mood to nurse a grievance rather than air it. I walked out
bare-headed. Terry came running after me with a coat.

'Put this on, Hugh,' she bade me.

'I don't want it,' I told her, and walked a couple of hundred
yards before I emptied the basin.

'What were you saying about electric light?' she asked
brightly on my return. 'Take off your jacket, boy, you're
wringing wet.'

'I am not,' I retorted.

'Could we make a water-wheel?' she asked after a pause.

'What's the good of talking about it?' I wanted to know.

'I would like to know, Hugh.'

All my resentment gathered itself against the plaintiveness
of her voice.

'And what's the use of planning as if we were to be here
for ever,' I cried.

Christ, and if she died, what hell of trifles I'd inhabit, recalling such words.

'That's true,' she agreed. 'Is it still coming down?'

'My peats will be washed away,' I complained.

'We can cut more.'

'It's easy for you to say that!' I exclaimed. 'It's not your labour that's wasting. If the rain came through the roof and messed up what you've done in the cave—'

'The peats mayn't be spoiled.'

'How could they escape being spoiled? This weather may carry on for months. A pretty pickle we'll be in then, without fuel for winter.'

All past and over, deep buried in the mind, ready to be remembered. Terry, I wish my heart would break and burst itself with grief for hurting you.

The weather faired this afternoon. We went out hoping to discover a cave or tented rocks near our own cave where our peats could be stowed in safety. The simplest course would be to build a stack either on the top of the rock near the moss or beside our cave but a stack large enough to outlast winter could not possibly be camouflaged with heathery turves; it is necessary to find a hiding-place.

The air, washed by the rain, was clear and fresh, and the farthest distances were bright in the sun; we looked through the limpid miles of air to the Cairngorms and the Monadhliahs; this air, like a sea of purifying waters, washed the green earth and the rocky hills. The ground was sopping wet; each shallow gully that we reached had its gurly torrent. We took off our shoes and stockings to splash barefoot through the burns and the velvet moss. I had never seen the country so verdant, under a bluer sky. The predominant yellows and browns of the moor seemed to have altered, as if the rain had changed them, or the air like glass altered their aspect.

We found no cave but Terry discovered an enormous boulder with a vertical face turned towards the cliff. We clambered to the top of the boulder where heather and grass had found root, to survey our realm. Our bare legs dangled

over the edge. It was so still and clear that we could hear
lambs bleating in the meadows of the Spey.

'Perhaps they're going to clip,' I said to Terry.

'Did you ever hear anything so clear and far away?' she
asked.

The noise of bleating came up to us from the distance
like the imagined sounds of a story.

'Like the goat in Daudet's story,' I said. 'Do you remember
when the wolf came, and every noise that the kid knew was
quiet, and its master gave up blowing his horn. "Come
home! come home!"'

'I've heard rooks like that,' she said, 'in the trees in a
valley.'

Our ears, which the noise of rain and streams and wind
had dulled, began to listen for the birds and beasts, and like
a wave the cry of whaups, the calling grouse, each sound
that rose from the moor or descended from the lift, welled
in upon us and we listened with all our souls; our hearts
were freed from their discontent by the large harmony of
freedom that our neighbours made around us in this place.

'We talk quite casually now about spending winter here,'
Terry said after a long silence.

'If we build our stack against the up side of this rock,'
I said, 'it would be hidden from everywhere unless some
one came right up to the cliff, and in that case we ourselves
would be seen. It's strange that we haven't seen a shepherd
amongst the sheep.'

'I can't worry or care about anything on a day like this,'
she answered.

'I feel as if I had lived all my life here,' I said.

'I was never happier than I am just now—it's wrong
of me,' she said, 'it's wicked to be so happy.'

'What's wrong in it?' I asked fiercely. 'Great God, what
hell is in the world when happiness is a crime? There's hope
for the world that has happiness in it. If it was all hate and
rage it would go like a heap of corruption mouldering itself
to nothing with its own rottenness.'

'Other people deserve happiness and haven't it,' she said

with a sigh. 'Hugh—you won't be very angry with me—you won't think I'm silly—'

I shook my head and answered, 'Not this day, Terry.'

She smiled at that.

'And other days?' she inquired.

'What were you going to say?' I asked.

'Hugh—I'd like to see our house. It's a foolish whim—and we've so much to do—'

'Why do you want to see the house?' I demanded.

'I can't get things out of my head, somehow,' she answered in a low voice. 'I lie awake, many a night, wondering what has happened, wondering what grief's abroad and us here, safe, us here, happy. It might be time for us to go back, Hugh. We might be able to do some good.'

'It's not the house you want to see,' I said.

'Yes, indeed I want to see our house, our own house, Hugh.'

'It's a long journey and there's risk of danger, Terry,' I told her. 'If you like I'll go and spy—'

'And leave me here alone! No, no, you couldn't do that. Why, it's not so very far. When can we go, Hugh?'

'When I've stacked my peats,' I told her grimly. 'I'm not taking any more risks with the weather.'

We sat for a space in silence, but it was with thoughts of our fellow-creatures, and the future, that our minds now engaged themselves; the singing birds in the birch wood sang their heedless song unheeded. We were mortal human folk, and all our work, all our home-making in the cave, all our happiness on this day of June, though it was sweet, did not divide us from our human fellows nor obliterate their woe.

OUR PEATS WERE less badly spoiled than we expected to find. We set them up on edge to dry and while those that I had already cut were weathering I delved a great many more. Terry took them from my spade and set them flat on bare rocks to grow firm. When they were fit to handle without breaking she brought them to the edge of the cliff above the boulder we had discovered. The rock here was barely thirty feet high, and if we could make a basket it would be easy to lower the peats at the end of a rope. I returned to the birch wood for a stout branch which I bent into a hoop two feet in diameter. We stretched a deer skin across the hoop and when ropes had been attached to it we had a primitive basket. Terry waited at the foot of the cliff to receive the loads I let down to her. She piled the peats beside the boulder ready for stacking. In a week of hard work we had a sizable stack, big enough, I reckoned, to last us six months. We decided to wait until after we had visited our house before we cut a further supply. We might not need them. We were loath to spend labour in vain.

Our backs were sore with bending over the peats. We had grown soft during our rainy days' idleness and we rested from working on the 19th of June. We slept in the sun, we wakened to inquire at each other, with many a supposition, how the peopled world had fared. We were both oppressed with a sense of crisis. The things we had left and fled to escape were never out of our minds since we decided to go to our house. Sometimes I said, forgetting the guns we heard, 'Suppose there was never any war, suppose we ran away from the shadow of a fear—' But

71

it did not require Terry's eyes to persuade me of what I dreaded to believe.

There have been times when our moods owed their birth to the weather; often when we are dull a change of weather instructs us in the cause of our lethargy. But on this sweet day, untroubled by wind or cloud, we were ill at ease for no cause save the anxiety of our minds; when we slept it was to waken with another question on our lips, a new imagining half-formed and dangerous in our heads.

'Another day past,' I said when night came. 'Another step towards the grave.'

'Why should I try to hide and make pretence?' Terry said suddenly. 'I'm half-distracted with anxiety, Hugh, and every moment a new dread pushes out the old—oh, Hugh! what dreadful things may have happened while we've been here.'

'I could go alone,' I said slowly. 'Who knows what has chanced?'

'I'm going too,' she said.

'We're lucky to have each other,' I murmured. 'What a poor wavering fool I'd be lacking you, Terry.'

'I'm glad you're happy with me,' she answered gently.

Before we fell asleep for the night, after we had turned a dozen times in our hammock, and lain still for minutes by force of will, to keep from waking the wakeful other, I sat up and whispered, 'Terry!'

'Hugh! are you waking? I've been longing to speak to you but I was loath to disturb you.'

'I can't sleep, Terry.'

'We slept too much through the day.'

'It's not that. My head won't stop thinking—'

'Och, sleep, my bairn, my dear,' she bade me. 'What is it troubles you, then?'

'Vain thoughts,' I said heavily.

I felt her hand touch my face lightly.

'Hush you and don't fret,' she murmured, 'sleep and forget pain; what is it troubles you? sleep, and be still.'

She began to sing, in her small thin voice:

Hush a ba birdie, croom, croom,
   Hush a ba birdie, croom,
The sheep are gane tae the silver wood,
And the cows are gane tae the broom, the broom.
Hush a ba birdie, croom, croom,
   Hush a ba birdie, bye,
The bells are ringing, the birds are singing,
The wild deer come galloping by.

'Am I bothering you, Hugh?' she asked after her song was done. 'Would you prefer me to keep quiet?'

She must have sensed me shaking my head, since she could not have seen, and I had no words. She began to sing again:

Hush and baloo, baby,
   Hush and baloo,
A' the lave's in their beds,
I'm hushing you.

Shortly I slept, to waken at dawn and creep out of the hammock. I was half-dressed when Terry sat up and said in a shrill frightened voice:

'Hugh! Where are you, Hugh?'

'Here,' I answered, going over to her.

She put her arms round my neck and clung to me.

'I must have been dreaming,' she whispered, 'I thought —I had a dreadful dream; Hugh—stay with me!'

'I'm here, I'm beside you,' I said. 'There's nothing to be afraid of, Terry.'

'It's to-day we're going,' she said.

'Yes,' I answered.

'Is it time to go?' she asked.

'Not till night,' I replied. 'I'm going out for a stag. We must have a full larder waiting for us when we come home.'

'I'm going with you,' she cried.

'But Terry—' I expostulated.

'Light the lamp,' she bade me; 'light the lamp till I see to put on my clothes. Take me with you to-day, Hugh.'

'You'll be tired to death,' I persisted. 'We've a long journey before us at the end of the day. There's a lot to do, getting ready—'

'I must go,' she said.

We were well out on the hill before daylight arrived. As we came to an eminence from which the valley of the Truim could be glimpsed as a dark narrow expanse between the hills a distant rumbling caught my attention.

'There are trains still,' I told Terry. 'Don't you hear it? Coming down from the summit of Drumochter Pass. Perhaps we'll catch sight of it.'

We sat down to wait.

'It's going at a hell of a pace,' I said. 'There didn't use to be an express at this hour.' As I spoke a glare of light swept into the valley and went hurtling northwards with a roar and a flare of fire-illumined steam. In a moment it was out of sight behind the Binion hill, and the noise receded towards Newtonmore, and our straining ears heard it no more. It was so calm we could hear a cock crowing in Dalwhinnie. So there were cocks betraying the dawn in our forsaken world. But scarcely had it crowed than we heard another train surmount Drumochter and accelerate downhill, to flame before us, and in its turn vanish.

We waited on our hill-top, as if struck to stone by expectation, and the golden day came up and gilded our peak, and every peak, but we had eyes for nothing save the trains that fled north before our gaze. Three of them followed the first, thundering down the slope, leaping into our view with a light that always took us by surprise though we were always waiting for it, vanishing from sound and sight into the emboskened valley of the Spey.

'God knows what that means,' I muttered.

'Easy to know what it means,' Terry said bitterly. 'War's no slugabed.'

We got up heavily to stalk a deer. A lucky chance saved us from much exertion. We killed a young beast all alone a mile beneath the peak whence we had viewed the trains. Terry hid in a rough hollow while I killed the deer and bled it.

'I wished we hadn't to kill it to-day,' she said.

I shrugged.

'We have to live,' I said.

She shouldered the rifle with an air of distaste.

The dawn was red and grey behind the eastern hills. Dawn, lief exorcist of care, lightened our hearts. As we went home we stumbled on a deer-calf in its couch.

'The lovely, lovely creature!' Terry cried, stooping over it.

'Don't lay a hand on it!' I warned her.

She looked up at me; her cheeks were wet.

'Would its mother forsake it?' she asked. 'Good morning, calfie, I'm glad I saw you.'

We spent the remainder of the morning in preparations for our journey. We boiled venison to carry with us, as well as a piece to eat when we arrived home again. We rolled blankets in our ground-sheet and fetched a slab of stone to cover the mouth of our cave. We talk, and say many things to hide what our minds are always saying. Our tongues ran like rivers as we worked, and all the while those trains were in our ears.

'I suppose lots of people would fancy that this sort of life was full of adventures, Hugh,' Terry remarked.

'I'm sure they would,' I agreed.

'They say folk in caves and wildernesses and desert islands escape all the trivialities of life.'

'I've heard so,' I agreed.

'What fools people are!' she cried. 'Folk in caves and desert islands must be far more commonplace and matter of fact than any one ever needs to be in a town. In a town you run to the shop at the corner—oh, my God, what is happening in towns?' she burst out.

'People take their notions of strange ways of life from books,' I suggested in an effort to save myself as well as her from thinking of the horror that would not be gainsaid.

'I wonder if there are still books being sold, Hugh?'

'Not mine, I'll be bound,' I returned.

'As soon as people discover that there's nothing martial in war they turn to books,' she said.

'Not to mine,' I insisted. 'What! read social histories when they've war!'

I could not be quiet, I could not hold my tongue, pretending that the world was as it had been.

'Maybe London's a heap like Babylon,' I burst out, 'and the hoodie crows glut themselves in the streets of Glasgow.'

'We'd have seen signs,' she answered slowly.

'Maybe it's all a false alarm,' I said.

'The guns? the trains?' she returned significantly.

'We'll soon know,' I said.

'What?' she demanded. 'What do you think we'll find, Hugh? God knows,' she answered herself. 'Why are we going?'

'Why are we here?' I cried wildly. 'We'll come back—'

'Yes, Hugh, we'll come back.'

'And live here, knowing nothing.'

'We might be in worse places, Hugh. And know worse things than nothing.'

'Our stores will go done at last—'

'We must get more.'

'More? How?'

'How? Take them if we can—go where they are—if we can't get them, live without them as the beasts do.'

'And die the way they do, for lack of food, for lack of warmth—die like beasts.'

'If I could make you patient, Hugh. You expect to-morrow to solve all our questions, to tell us all that's happened. It won't do that, Hugh. We'll see our house, we'll gather some of the things we ought to have brought originally—'

'We're bound to discover—' I broke in.

'What?' she asked with scorn. 'That we've done right? Don't you know that already? If we haven't done right, nothing will ever change it. All you'll see there,'—she extended her arm to the north—'is the backwash of trouble; all you'll hear is rumour as various as our own minds make.'

'Nothing more, nothing at all?' I said. 'Then we can stay, and doubt, and never be sure, here till we die.'

'If I could save you from building up hopes of finding more than we'll ever find out,' she said, 'it would make me glad even if we discovered—even if we discovered deadly things.'

'Then we had better stay where we are. At least we'll see signs of war—we'll see trains—'

'Must you have signs?' she demanded. 'Must you put your hands in the holes of the nails, before you believe?'

I stared out over the signless land.

'I can't help the way I'm made,' I said at last. 'I can't feel here, in my heart, that the thing has happened, until I see its mark.'

'The mark is in your face and on your heart already, Hugh.'

'To live in doubt—' I whispered.

'Hugh,' she said in low tones. 'It wasn't merely to escape from war and conscription we came here, not to avoid mere facts like murder and outrage and poison gas.'

'What then?' I inquired. 'Was it self-begotten fears that chased us? Were we so cowardly?'

'Out of the world that uses such means and thinks such thoughts,' she said, 'out from amongst men who hate each other—'

'Fleeing from the wrath to come,' I quoted mockingly. 'Discreet but not valiant. So we're tuppenny evangelists awaiting the dawn of peace, hey?'

'Fleeing from the wrath that is,' she said.

'And all the captains and all the kings and all the great men shall hide themselves,' I rattled on. 'We've certainly rocks enough to call down on our heads, Terry. The new Armageddon.'

'Hugh!' she pleaded.

'Terry!' I returned defensively.

'And if there's no war, and all's peaceful,' she said, composing herself, 'we'll go back to our house.'

I looked at her without speaking.

'And stand on the lip of hell,' she went on drearily, 'waiting for whispers, waiting for war, war more horrible the longer it's delayed.'

'No,' I said in a low voice. 'So here we sit till the millennium,' I said a moment later. 'What if it comes in winter time, Terry, and we can't get down for storm, like old Macdonald of Glencoe in *his* day of pacification, or we can't hear the sound of the call when the Prince of Peace sounds his rally for the noise of wind and storm?'

'I think we should be making ready,' she said in a breaking voice. Then she cried, 'Hugh! Hugh! it rends my heart to hear you mocking and bitter.'

'Does it gladden my own?' I asked. I could say nothing to comfort her. I stood staring at the ground like one transfixed by the shafts of despair while she went silently away to put on her shoes for the journey.

We prepared for the going with mechanical care. I took our ammunition from the cave and hid it in a cleft of the rock. I cleaned the lenses of my telescope and set out the .22 and slipped the bolt of the .303 into my pocket. If we returned to find an intruder I had rather not meet him armed with our own weapon.

We departed in the twilight of the 20th of June. It was a rare evening. Many trout were rising on Loch Coulter; we passed sheep that scarcely lifted their heads to look at us, so greedily were they feeding with their lambs amongst them. No sheep was shorn. We crossed the road, we climbed into the triangle of low hills which divides the valley of the Truim from the Spey, and on the approach of morning we lay down amongst birch trees, in the security of a wilderness of rocks above Glentruim to sleep until night made journeying safe once more. There, high over the Truim's noisy undiscernible stream, we saw the well-known valley, and heard cattle lowing, and a car went down the north road. It was like the quietest day of other years. When the sun descended we rolled up our bundle. Our route was dangerous amongst trees and rocks and we made slow progress; clouds of midges tormented us. We did not reach our house until past midnight. We could not see a light anywhere in the valley. The absence of lights seemed ominous; yet it was late, and country folk go early to bed, saving their lamps: midsummer had never lights that I could recall, save the sky, but I was afraid when I saw nothing but darkness in the glen. I searched in vain for a glimmer that would show men were awake in their houses.

'Hugh!' Terry whispered when we came to the familiar gate. It was open. 'We must have forgotten to lock the gate,' she said under her breath.

'Perhaps the postman left it open,' I returned in the same voice. Her hand touched and clasped mine. We tiptoed up the path. I thought that the door was open and I checked my pace.

'Are you seeing anything, Hugh?' Terry whispered. 'Can you make out—what are you seeing?'

'Nothing,' I lied, with my eyes fixed on the open door.

'I can't bear to go farther,' she muttered. 'I'm frightened.'

'There's nothing to fear,' I said gently. 'We've come too far to go back.'

I was afraid to death myself but not with fear of danger. Terry let go my hand to fall on her knees beside a flower-plot.

'I'm going to take plants back with me,' she said, and then, 'It's all trampled down!' she cried. She stared about her until she perceived the black gap of the open door.

'We locked the door,' she said.

'I'm not certain if we did,' I began. 'In the hurry—'

'We did! I know we did! Hugh, the kitchen window's broken.'

There was something horrible about the silence of the house, about our petrified silent vigil at the door of our own house. I felt suddenly desolate.

'We should go away,' I said in a choked voice, but when I spoke anger took hold of me, and I ran to the door and went in. A foul air greeted me. Terry came at my heels.

I knew my way through the rooms in darkest pitch night and I hurried from the lobby to the kitchen. My feet made a grating noise on the floor as I walked, and I heard broken glass break under my boots.

'What's happened here?' I asked aloud. 'What's happened here?' I demanded again of the barren air.

'Light a match, Hugh,' Terry told me. When the light flared up I heard her cry, 'Oh!'

Our first impulse was to run away and leave for ever that fouled gutted house that was our home. We stayed to glut our rage and lacerate our hurt, going from room to room, calling each other to see each new defilement that we found. We fell on our knees on the filthy floors to turn over the broken rubbish gathered there, to pick fragments from the heap of muck and say, 'This was our picture,' and, 'That was your party dress, Terry,' and, 'Don't you remember when we bought this, Hugh?' Everything we owned lay on the floor, trampled, smeared with the dirt of miry boots, broken. The very walls were smeared with muck and our chairs had been torn to bits to make firewood. The fireplaces were overflowing with ashes and bits of wood, bits of picture-frames, bits of trunks, charred papers. Dishes and bottles broken into fragments littered the kitchen floor. Our books met us everywhere we moved. I struck matches mechanically, holding each match until it burnt my fingers, then lighting the next and putting the burnt stump carefully back into the box as I had learned to do on the hill or in our cave. Terry came to me with a little broken Dresden shepherdess in her cupped hands.

'It's almost not broken at all,' she said in a queer voice. Her face was haggard, her eyes wild. They went out as the match I held went out, and then they were before me again.

'Throw it away,' I told her harshly, 'throw the damned thing away.'

'Will we go now?' she said in the same strained voice. 'Will we go now?' she insisted in rising tones. 'There's nothing you want to take with you, Hugh?'

'Nothing that's been touched—' I managed to say, and could find no more words.

'There's my good frock,' she cried, pouncing on a tattered fragment of silk on the floor.

'It's time for us to go,' I said in a miserable voice. 'Give me your hand, Terry.'

'Oh, but I can see the way,' she returned. 'Are you there, Hugh? Don't leave me.'

I took her hand. I could feel the pieces of the china image in her clenched fist.

'Are you taking this with you?' I asked.

'My shepherdess!' she said in surprised tones.

'Terry!' I cried. I was distracted, scarcely knowing what I did.

'What's the matter, Hugh?' she asked in the same astonished voice. 'Come, it'll soon be day, we must go, have you the rifle?'

'Terry!' I said, catching her by the arms, 'Terry! what's the matter with you?'

'You're hurting me,' she complained. 'Let go my arm, Hugh.'

I could dimly perceive her pinched features in the June darkness. She struggled to be free, but I held her still.

'You're hurting me,' she said angrily a second time. A moment later her voice fell to a childish complaint, 'Oh, my head!' She gave up struggling and began to sob. I held her in my arms with her face close to me. The wild-briar on our wall, broken though its branches were, made a faint sweet familiar smell. Soon she fell from sobbing to tears, and then she murmured, 'I'm sleepy, Hugh, oh, so sleepy; take me home, Hugh.'

We returned to our cave, walking all day without attempting to hide. Terry was asleep on her feet long before we reached the cave. Helping her occupied me. Sometimes I carried her over miry ground and rocks and burns. I staggered to and fro like a drunk man. I could scarcely waken her when I laid her down.

So we came home. We lay down to sleep, but I could not sleep. I rose at dusk to make a meal for Terry and myself. She wakened too, her face all swollen with tears. I can hear her in the cave behind me, cooking and cleaning as I write.

I have no tears. *My* eyes are dry. Oh, Terry, Terry, our walls are broken and the garden spoiled.

Memory has no surcease. Each battered trinket on the filthy floor confronts me. This longest day will never end.

IT IS THE FIFTH of July. In an hour or so we shall have spent three full months here.

'It doesn't seem like months,' Terry said when I reminded her of the date of our coming.

'It scarcely feels like time at all,' I agreed. I had a momentary vision of our tiny figures struggling under their load across the moor in that April night.

'The nights are beginning to draw in,' Terry went on. 'I can see a difference in the light already, Hugh.'

'Yes,' I said with a sigh, 'the year's going downhill now; we must attend to our firewood though the weather is so hot. Soon it'll be autumn; we can't count on dry weather after August. And then winter—I *hate* the turn in the day, Terry. June's so fine—'

'No horse-flies and no thunder,' she assented with a smile. 'Those brutes of clegs! I'm all swollen with their bites!'

We have done no work to-day. Our peats are cut and stacked, in spite of the clegs, and we are content to rest.

We went down to Loch Coulter in the breathless morning to bathe before the heat of the day arrived. I had the .22 with me. I carry it habitually whenever I leave the cave. We heard black cock drumming on a green lawn amongst the birches. I slipped away to stalk the birds, leaving Terry splattering in the shallows of a sandy cove. I got near enough to my quarry to see how they danced; with their fan tails spread out like a turkey cock's and their wings trailing the ground they advanced and retreated, head to head; they danced and drummed; sometimes a pair would face each other with their heads lowered to the ground and their eyes

82

a couple of inches apart, until one of the birds gave way, and
their see-saw backwards and forwards dance recommenced.

They heard me in the brushwood and flew away. I was
not deeply vexed. We had meat enough in the cave.

We are growing familiar with the habits of our neighbours.
We know where the black cock dance. I have seen the eagles
make homewards for their eyrie in the Little Durc, and
followed them until I came to the head of that canyon and
saw the nest, and smelled the stench of rotting game. I
know the solitary hill-side trees where hoodies nest, and
have nested perhaps for a century; the ravens make their
home in the rock above our cave. We never walk barefoot
in the birch wood since I killed an adder, slender and vicious
and as full of fat as a pike, beside an ant-heap there.

'It gives me a shudder to look at it,' Terry declared when
I brought it for her to see. 'What possessed you to bring it
here, Hugh?'

'Don't you like it?' I teased her. 'I think it's pretty. And
full of fat.'

'Why should pike and snakes and wicked brutes like them
be so well lined?' she wanted to know.

'The wicked grow fat,' I said, and laughed.

'You're not very fat yourself, Hugh,' she declared, looking
at me with a critical eye. 'But you're looking well, I never saw
you looking so healthy. You're as brown as a berry—'

When the sun went down to-day we made a fire of sticks
outside the cave and ate a little.

'If this hot weather continues we'll save our stores,' Terry
declared.

'It's almost a fortnight since we came back,' I said slowly.

'Yes,' she returned, 'a long fortnight, long in passing.
Looking back, our journey's like the bad weather in June,'
she said a little later, 'dark and miserable—and past.'

'It's past then?' I inquired, looking intently at her quiet
face.

'It was sore, sore for a while,' she murmured. 'Our poor
house—it did us good to see it though it hurt, Hugh.'

'It brought us to earth,' I asserted grimly. 'It taught us

that our game was earnest. We were like children playing at a picnic.'

'Oh, it did more, far more than that, Hugh,' she said.

We were dead beat when we reached the cave after our journey. We slept uneasy hours and wakened more tired than when we lay down. Our bones ached, our minds were drunk with fatigue, we moved in a stupor.

Everything I did was wrong and clumsy. When I reached out my hand to lift a pot or a cup I fumbled, and my nerves were on edge expecting the thing I caught to fall from my grasp and break. The least hindrance put me in a rage, and from sudden temper I fell into silence whose outward appearance was surly, whose inward cause and accompaniment was misery. Terry moved through the cave like a ghost, wan and silent and apprehensive-eyed. I would have given the world to be able to speak, to comfort her and unburden my own trouble. I was spell-bound to silence and the best I could fashion my lips to say was, 'We must count our stores. It's past time we estimated how long we can live on them.'

I laid out our hoard of boxes and parcels in the middle of the cave and Terry reckoned how much they held and how long the essential things like flour and salt would last us. We began by setting aside the stuff of which we had sufficient to last an indefinite time. The future was so uncertain and overclouded that a year ahead seemed like old age to youth, a fabulous distance away.

Our ammunition came first in this category. If I kept on using it as carefully as I had in the past, I could not conceive an end to it; I suppose we were desperately avoiding thought of the far future. If we planned years ahead, we were dooming ourselves irrevocably to a life of exile.

'We needn't look so far ahead,' I answered when Terry asked how long the ammunition would last. 'Every other thing that makes life sufferable will be finished long before the ammunition is used up.'

'Very well,' she agreed. 'There's not much point in

planning for the distant future when a thousand things may happen to upset our arrangements.'

'How much salt have we?' I inquired.

We had sufficient to carry us on to spring at our present rate of use, but, as I pointed out, in winter we would have storms and we must salt a store of meat against them.

'And how we are going to do it is beyond my imagination,' I went on, 'for we have neither tub nor barrel.'

'Can't we dry-salt the meat and hang it from the rafters?' Terry asked. 'Or if the winter's hard meat will keep in the snow.'

Our flour likewise was enough for seven or eight months. 'We've been using a quarter of tea a week,' Terry said. 'We have no more than three pounds remaining. We'll miss our tea when it's done.'

'Then we must drink water and spare the tea,' I declared. 'What about sugar?'

'We haven't used a great deal,' she replied. 'The condensed milk has eked it out, but the milk's practically used up.'

'It's a luxury, anyway,' I declared.

'No doubt it is,' she agreed, 'but lots of things which are luxuries in themselves become necessities when they are all lacking. We can live without sugar and butter and vegetables, I don't say we'll starve while we have meat and flour, but I don't believe we can keep healthy. Our jam's a luxury—'

'How much is left?' I interrupted.

'Three jars; we used it heavily for a while. You were supping it with a spoon, Hugh.'

'I never did!' I declared indignantly, and was forced to smile. 'How did you find out?' I asked.

'You forgot to clean the spoon,' she told me.

'It was very wicked and thoughtless of me,' I said. 'But oh, Terry, I was so sick of meat! meat! meat! I thought I'd die for something sweet.'

'I'm not blaming you,' she continued, 'but I was counting on the jam to keep us healthy through the winter.'

'We can make more,' I informed her gleefully.

'Can we?' she cried. 'Is that true? Is there fruit hereabouts?'

'Yes, cranberries,' I said, 'and probably crowberries and blaeberries too, and I saw the averans in full flower on the top of the Farrow; we'll get them in the autumn if the frost doesn't take them. There'll be heaps of rowans and we could go down to the Spey where the rasps grow. You need a lot of sugar for rowans—'

'If we have enough sugar to preserve them, the sourer they are the better for us,' Terry declared. 'That's a great load off my mind.'

When we concluded the tale of our stores we knew that we had as much salt and flour as would suffice us until spring.

'Then they're likely to outlast us,' I commented bitterly when Terry told me her conclusion.

'The biscuits and the butter are nearly done,' she went on.

We have ten dozen eggs preserved. The ham is mostly all eaten. Our vegetables are finished. The potatoes grew soft and Terry had to throw most of them away. 'We've more of some things than we had to begin with,' Terry said.

'That's a blessing,' I said ironically.

'Why are you angry with me, Hugh?' she asked. 'Why do you speak to me as you do?'

'How do I speak to you?' I inquired with defensive roughness.

'Are you tired of me?' she asked in low tones.

I stood staring at the floor of the cave with its litter of tins. Though it drove a knife into my heart to see her sad and hurt I could not help hurting her, and I waited a long minute before I muttered, 'No.'

'What about tobacco?' she said in a strangled voice.

'It'll go done. Oh, what does it matter, what does anything matter?'

'We can live well enough until spring,' she continued in the same voice.

'And what then?' I demanded.

I felt her hand on my arm, and her voice, full of tears, asked gently:

'Is it the house, Hugh?' Then she came near me and said: 'Look at me, Hugh.'

I raised my eyes unwillingly. My cheeks were burning hot.

'My dear, my heart, my love, my only love,' she whispered. 'I wish I could help you—can't you tell me—'

'What'll I tell you?' I cried wildly, 'that every mortal thing is drear and hopeless and my heart's dead in my body, dead as a stone, and I wish I was dead too.'

'Hush, hush,' she entreated, 'we've each other still.'

'How can I hush?' I raged. 'We're here for ever, Terry, we'll never escape, we'll starve and rot in this den, this hole in the rocks. Was it for this we were born, to live like beasts without hope?'

'We'll go and cut more peats,' she said gently. 'Soon it'll be better, soon we'll be done with remembering the pain of the thing that's in our heads, a little time changes the worst things out of their shape and makes us masters again in the house of our own minds.'

I was deserted suddenly by the raging energy, compounded of anger and pain, which possessed me since we returned from our journey; it made me fly from one task to another, now cutting a bench of peats in the bog, again counting the time our stores would last, then trailing roots of bog-fir from their mossy resting-place beside the loch; it left me and I grew so tired that I could scarcely stand on my feet.

'What's the good?' I asked wearily when Terry said we ought to go to our peats.

'Are you tired, Hugh?' she asked.

'I'm blind with tiredness,' I answered. 'Tired and sick.'

'Then rest,' she urged. 'You've been overdoing it of late. No human being could stand up to the pace you were setting yourself.'

'Oh, Terry, Terry!' I cried. 'It's a dreadful thing to be outcasts and fugitives.'

'Other people have been fugitives before us,' she said.

'We'll go to the peats,' I muttered.

We climbed to the hill-top and I cut the turf from a

new bank of peat. The day was hot but fresh with a brisk wind from the south. There were as yet no clegs on the high ground to plague us and make the heat of summer a scourge instead of a pleasure. The spade went smoothly into the black moist bank, the sun shone in its azure world, the wind came sweetly over peaks that still kept snow in their north corries facing us. My spirits rose, gloom lightened, and as my strength returned and I worked I felt the content of the summer day that reigned over our country enter my heart. And Terry, with a red handkerchief knotted at the corners on her head to keep her black hair from her eyes and the force of the sun from her brain, bare-armed and bare-legged and eager, ran back and fore with peats in her arms to spread them out to dry. I commenced to feel free from my nightmarish oppression. I could think clearly. In a moment of realization when I knew that I was escaping from the horror which preyed on me I let the spade fall from my hands. The wind was like water on my arms. I breathed the air like a blind man who with restored sight gazes on the clear outlined world. Terry cried, 'Isn't it grand, up here, on the top of the world!'

'It's very fine,' I answered gravely. She began to laugh like a happy child and dance amongst the peats, waving her bare peat-smeared arms over her head.

We bathed in Loch Coulter; we lay at the mouth of our cave to attend night's summer shade; we saw the rough hills climb up against the sky and it grew dark enough for stars to shine. There are moments when misery departs that require no voice; we waited in silence until night reached its deepest, though it was only twilight still.

'Our garden was no more our own than this,' Terry said.

'This!' I cried, startled. 'We made our garden, Terry—'

'Poor garden!' she sighed. 'No one watering it in this heat!'

'And all the weeds spreading like fire,' I took her up. 'I wonder what creatures broke into the house, Terry.'

She did not answer.

'Will we ever leave here?' I asked a few minutes later.

'I don't know,' she said. 'I scarcely care. We are free, here's no fret nor rumours. Are you happier, Hugh?'

'Happy? I don't know—I'm not unhappy.'

'You were unhappy.'

'What else could I be? Oh but we shouldn't have been so weak, Terry, we shouldn't have let it overwhelm us. We came back without a single thing to help us. After all our planning, after that long journey, we came back without one of the things we went for—'

'Excepting resolution,' she interrupted quietly.

'We didn't find out anything,' I continued.

We knew, without any evidence of our eyes and ears, but by the instruction of instinct merely, that it was not the state of our house by itself which appalled us and drove us back to the hills. Our house was a portent of the world. That blind squalid fate which happened to it, and involved us, was general, though we had no proof to give our minds, assuring them they thought truly, or to tell our hearts that the woe which lay on them was justly felt. When we saw our house we knew, suddenly and without doubt, that it had fellows more horridly destroyed, and we had fellows too. We were afraid; we were overwhelmed by the knowledge of events that we had never heard of, but for which our house stood as a token. I remembered the lightless valley of the Spey.

On this day of passing June, throughout this night, we escaped into the country where the sun and the moor existed by themselves; and in this place, divorced from the land of men, we escaped from fear and unhappiness. We were as the wild creatures of our wild country.

WE HAVE BEEN gathering blaeberries for jam this evening in the birch wood above Loch Coulter. Things ripen late here. We must be thirteen hundred feet above sea-level and the flush of ripe berries will not come for several days yet. Nevertheless we find bushes hung with swollen blue-dusted fruit in sheltered hollows exposed to the south and we have grown prudent enough to gather what fruit we can at the earliest moment of ripening. If rain comes unexpectedly the berries that are ripe will be spoiled for jam. Fruit is not so plentiful that we can afford to let any go to waste.

We were very imprudent lately. When we arrived home from our house, running to escape in broad daylight, we were past caring whether we were seen. And even after we arrived at the cave we continued to act as if nothing mattered except our unhappiness. We went out to cut peats in a rage of energy that proved no anodyne as if there were no other people in the world but ourselves. That first stage passed, yet we grew no more cautious, for we were filled with exaltation as blind as our despair.

I shudder now to think of the risks we ran. We cut our peats at midday. I scoured the country for game at noon. We spent every daylight hour in the open, as if we craved to be discovered.

Clegs were the instruments of caution, and halted our thoughtless bravado. They appeared in the first days of July, before we finished working in the peat-moss. They did not punish me so viciously as they hurt Terry. Their bites raised lumps on her and their poison, together with the aversion they created, made her sick, while I took no

great ill-effect from their venom. In spite of my immunity I
dreaded them fully as much as she did. They filled me with
loathing and, ridiculous as it seems, with fear. A single cleg
aiming itself at my arm was enough to make me fling down
whatever I had in my hand to beat the insect away with crazy
gestures.

The clegs made the moss untenable through the day.
Each peat as it dried seemed to make a resting-place for
multitudes of the brutes, and at our approach they rose in
ravenous swarms. We retreated and ventured out only at
dusk when midges made a lesser nuisance, or in the cool
of daybreak.

We had been exalted, too highly exalted as we had been
too deeply depressed, when we emerged from the misery
induced by our journey. The clegs tempered our new delight
in the country and in our freedom. When they had driven
us to work by night it occurred to us that we should never
have been abroad through the day. We had been reckless
and foolish. One grey morning, as I was lowering peats
in the basket, I bethought me of the risks we had been
running, and I hurried down to speak to Terry.

'Is anything wrong?' she asked anxiously, coming to
meet me.

'Terry!' I cried, 'what in the world have we been thinking
about, these past weeks? Some one must have seen us.
It's just dawned on me—I was thinking about the clegs
forcing us to work at night—we *ought* to have been
working by night.'

'I had the very same thought,' she returned. 'But if we
were seen we'd know by now—'

'If we weren't seen we've been lucky beyond our deserts,'
I declared.

Now everything we had done seemed conspicuous and
rash. I insisted on thatching the peat-stack with turves,
although anyone who came near enough to discern the stack
must inevitably find our cave. We have laughed since these
careful days at our excess of caution. We broke down the
sides of our peat-moss to make my excavation look as much

like the untidy work of nature as possible. We deferred bringing fir roots home until we found a secure hiding-place for them. Terry plotted a strict routine of hours, for meals and work and sleep.

We kept strictly to her arrangement for almost a week. We slept from midday to dusk. Then we ate a light meal of a fried pancake made with flour and a gull's egg; we allowed ourselves one egg a day. We drank a cup of weak tea. When the blaeberries started to ripen we added a dish of fruit to this our first meal of the day.

The nights of early July were never so dark that we could not see to work out of doors; even when the valleys were dim a luminance in the sky made the peaks visible; one could have seen to read small print by the light of the sky shining on the hill-top where we cut our peats. The sun's progress past north to its rising was marked by gaudy colours all round the northern horizon.

Sometimes we took a piece of boiled venison with us, in case we grew hungry, but most nights we worked without more food until dawn warned us to leave the moss. I remained for a while cutting peats by myself while Terry descended to cook. In the new spirit of caution that gripped us we cut a vast quantity of peats beyond what we were ever likely to use. But, we said, no one knew how soon winter might come on us, nor how long it would last.

We had an appetite for dinner. Game formed the staple of this meal. Sometimes Terry pot-roasted a bit of venison haunch and made a sort of Yorkshire pudding to accompany the meat; generally she stewed the venison; we had venison and grouse, blue hill hares and an occasional rabbit, black-cock, snipe, duck, plover and roe-deer. We had no lack of quantity and variety so far as meat was concerned. As soon as the blaeberries ripened we added them to our dinner. Terry often made soup of a bone; we hunted the country round for green stuff to put in the broth.

Our garden of nettles which grew over the ruins of an old house was quickly stripped. We cooked the nettles like cabbage and used the water in which they were boiled amongst our soups. The nettle-pottage tasted as sweet as cabbage, but it came to an end. We tried many queer messes thereafter, young grass in the soup, birch leaves cooked like cabbage. We attempted to eat the latter dish once only. But when we flung away the mess of boiled birch leaves I recalled a trick of my boyhood. I made slots in the bark of some birch trees and collected the spilling sap that flowed from these cuts in milk-tins nailed to the trunks of the trees. We supped the sap with a teaspoon as if it was medicine, and felt that it was doing us good.

'Spring's the time for the sap,' I told Terry.

'We'll need it then,' she said.

We dug up the small nuts that grow at the root of a white-flowered plant on grassy slopes, as I used to when I was a boy.

The arrival of ripe blaeberries saved us from worrying about scurvy.

'And after them come crowberries.' I said, 'and cranberries then, and cloudberries. Terry, before we lack we'll go down to the fields at Kinlochlaggan or Laggan Bridge and steal turnips, like our neighbours the deer.'

'We'll have to,' she said simply.

When we had eaten dinner we bathed in Loch Coulter. If there was time to spare before bright day arrived we set a line for pike. We took food once again in mid-morning. We gave ourselves a precious bannock of oatcake spread thinly with jam or thickly with deer-fat, or we had scones that Terry baked on the griddle. We drank water.

We often say, in wonder-struck tones after a plain bare meal, that we never felt so well in all our lives before.

The strict routine lasted less than a week. We found, as we did months ago, that this life does not permit the unyielding governance of a time-table. We have gradually made our routine elastic again, though we keep generally to our framework of hours. We take no risks. The dread of discovery is very present in our minds though we scarcely know why we are afraid to be seen or what discovery entails. Our first instinct, when anything surprises us, is to hide.

'We are like wild animals,' I said when Terry marvelled at our continual alertness. 'Always watching, always scared, always ready to run and hide. No one will surprise us now, Terry, we've got back old lost instincts for danger.'

'We'll be pretty objects if we go back amongst people,' I went on. 'We'll be dodging and starting and turning our heads every minute of the day.'

'We won't like it, when we go back,' she took me up.

'How?' I wanted to know.

'You may hate solitude, Hugh, but it changes you. When we go back we'll be like country folk in a city. We'll be crowded, and overlooked, and choked for lack of room. We won't take well to a house—'

'Like the tinkers,' I laughed.

'Choking for lack of room to breathe,' she went on seriously.

'*If* we go back,' I interrupted her. 'And if we go back there may not be so many people round us to crowd us as there used to be.'

We stared at each other, and I could read in her eyes, as she read in mine, the fear and despair that we strove daily to hide even from ourselves. We could not cheat ourselves all the time, and even when we seemed to forget the reason for our escape, those guns we heard spoke to our secret minds, and the thought of war disturbed our inmost thoughts.

'What are we slaving for?' I cried. 'What are we arranging and planning for? I tell you it's to kill thought that we're racing and hurrying, Terry—to kill thought!'

I gave up picking blaeberries this evening to watch her where she sat under a rock curtained with berry bushes. She sat there picking the fruit with an air of complete absorption. For every berry that went into her dish half a dozen found their way to her mouth. I grew suddenly afraid of losing her, and such an anguish of terror seized me that my strength went from me and my heart was turned to ice. I watched her and I could not speak nor move.

She turned her face towards me. Her startled look recalled my wits and I strove to smile. Her mouth and cheeks were

blue with the blue dust of the blaeberries and when she
opened her mouth to laugh she showed a tongue and teeth
all black and red with the dye and juice of the fruit.

'Why! what is it, Hugh?' she asked, gazing steadily
at me.

I smiled as best I could. Then I gave up pretending. I
let my head fall on my hands and surrendered myself up to
desolate thoughts. In an instant she was kneeling beside me.

'Hugh! Hugh!' she cried, 'are you ill?'

'I'm all right,' I articulated, raising my head with an effort.

'You're as white as a ghost,' she went on. 'What's the
matter, Hugh?'

My tongue was loosened and I babbled like a child, crying,
'Terry, don't leave me, never leave me, Terry.'

'There, there, don't be afraid,' she comforted me. 'I'm
here; Terry's here beside you; what harm can come to
us? What nonsense is this you've got into your poor foolish
head? What, is this all you've gathered? Look what I've
got!'

'You haven't such an awful lot,' I muttered.

'I have so, pounds more than you, anyway. Come on,
hurry up, and we'll fill our dishes and go home for supper.
You're hungry, I know what's wrong with you. What'll we
have for supper, fried trout or baked pike? I wish you
could see your face, Hugh. Were you eating berries by the
handfuls?'

But when I glimpsed her face while she thought my eyes
were turned the other way I saw there the same appalled
look that I knew my own eyes betrayed.

WE WALKED WITH Duncan almost as far as the
Dalwhinnie road. We would have gone farther if he let
us. He forced us to stop, he walked from us, and while
we watched his retreating figure he did not halt or even
turn his head.

'Good-bye and God keep you,' he said.

'Don't go, Duncan,' Terry implored, 'stay here with us,
we've room and food—'

He smiled and held out his hand.

'Every one his own way,' he said gently.

'When will we see each other again?' I asked in a strained
voice.

He looked at me fixedly and said, 'Be good to her, Hugh.'

All at once he seized my hand and shook it; he bent
down and kissed Terry's cheek, and said, 'You must not
come farther,' and turned and walked away.

We stood side by side, gazing after him without a word
to say.

'I never saw a man walk so beautifully,' Terry whispered.
'He knows he'll never come back,' she said, speaking with
difficulty.

He reached the fence and crossed it, his tall figure vanished
in a dip of the road.

'We'll never seen him again!' she cried. 'Oh! oh! why
should it happen! why should it be!' And she fell to crying
and sobbing.

I let her alone. I could not sweeten the moment for myself,
far less comfort another. I saw Duncan climb from the dip
in the road. He halted his stride for the first time since he
left us. He stood by the roadside fence and bending over it

with both hands on the top wire he looked across the moor.
A hare that he had lifted got on its hind legs on the top of a
hillock to stare at us. We waited a long time, watching until
Duncan returned to his way. He showed no sign of seeing
us. We also went back the way we came.

We have gone over and over every moment of his visit,
from the instant of his arrival out of the morning mist in
the gorge beneath our cave. He came on us by surprise.
We had been carrying fir roots to the cave from the head of
Loch Coulter since dawn. We were resting half-way up the
steep ascent from the gully when Duncan showed himself
on the edge of the mist below us. I had as ever my rifle with
me. It was to my shoulder and trained on the approaching
figure before I realized what I was doing. It comes to my
shoulder automatically now when I see a moving creature,
but this was the first time I aimed it with deadly intent at
a man.

We have rehearsed every word he spoke, and all we said
to him. We told him what we had done, showing him this
clever makeshift, asking him to admire that other thing.
He sat and smiled, and kept silent; we were afraid to
ask outright, to discover what he knew. When he spoke
we listened with bated breath, dreading to discover what
he dreaded to tell, and never told. We listen still, and look
after him, towards the way he has gone. It is not difficult to
remember every word he spoke. When they are told, and
told again, we recall his looks, his eyes, the fashion of his
silence.

We tell ourselves, we cry that he was happy, happy with
us, could he not stay! he was happy while the days he stole
to give us ran their course. He sat for hours by the cave door
following Terry with his eyes, smiling when she looked at
him, evading our questions.

But when we tell each other that he was happy here, we
think then that he went away, we could not keep him from
going. Should we stay when he has gone? Oh, my mind is
vague and filled with doubts. I tell Terry that his mind was
made up to go and nothing we could say or do would have

weighed with him. In spite of argument we cannot escape the feeling that there is something we could have done or left undone to keep him with us, and save our friend. Or else we should have gone too.

We went back to our cave, alone now, quite alone. The roots I was carrying up the hill when Duncan arrived were lying on the brae where I dropped them to snatch my rifle from my shoulder. I began to gather up the fir. My finger was on the trigger to kill my friend.

'It was touch and go,' I said to Terry. 'What would have happened if it was a stranger? My finger was hard on the trigger.'

'But it wasn't a stranger,' she replied.

'It wasn't a stranger,' I said with a sigh. 'I can't get rid of the feeling—'

'What feeling?' she inquired when I paused.

'That I'm a murderer in my heart, that I'm like the thing we ran from to escape.'

'You'd never have done it,' she said gently. 'You think you would, when you look back you imagine it was just chance that saved you. You'd not have done it, Hugh. There's more than chance.'

We came to the cave. We spread out the things Duncan brought for us on the floor. There were apples and sweets and lettuce from a deserted garden he passed, flour and sugar, salt and a bottle of whisky, a rifle with ammunition and a telescope and a knife.

He did not tell us to come home.

'Is it a good rifle?' Terry asked.

'Too good,' I answered. 'His own.'

'He wouldn't have stayed whatever we did,' she cried all of a sudden, and then she appealed to me with, 'Would he, Hugh?'

I shook my head.

'Don't you remember this telescope?' I asked. 'He was given it—his name's on the case.'

He had given us what he would have given his friends if he was about to die.

She commenced to gather the gifts and stow them away.

'Give me the glass,' she said. 'It used to hang by his chair.'

She took the telescope and polished its black worn leather case with her sleeve and hung it beside the fire.

We felt as if the last links that tied us to our fellows were being broken as she laid aside each relic of Duncan's visit. We were outcast indeed.

'You're looking white and tired,' I told her. 'Hadn't you better rest?'

She moved about the cave, putting out her hands to set things in their proper places; she moved like an automaton. Her face was white and tired.

She let her hands fall by her side.

'I can't rest,' she said in a small voice.

'You must rest,' I answered.

'If I bide still my mind torments me,' she cried. 'The only hope I have of peace is when I work. Oh, Hugh! I can't get Duncan out of my mind. He'll never come back! He knows he'll never come back, never no more!'

'A man must go the way set for him,' I muttered.

She looked at me and did not speak.

'Day and night,' she said drearily, 'day and night I think of him and all folk. Can't you see them, Hugh!' she cried hysterically, 'with their faces to the sky, waiting—and hunger killing them, no strength left to move but falling down, lying on the ground with their faces to the sky, waiting—'

'Hush, my dear,' I whispered, going near her; 'what use is it to think like that? It'll send us mad if we let such thoughts prey on us.'

'Oh, but I think I am going mad, often and often I think the thoughts of my head will break my reason,' she said with horrid clarity. Her voice was clear and reasonable but her face was twisted with pain and her eyes were like those of a hurt brute in a snare. As I watched her the pupils of her eyes contracted and her eyes grew hard and shallow with fear.

'Terry!' I implored, 'Terry! for pity's sake—'

I could scarcely find breath to voice my prayer to her. Fear choked my breath and laid harsh fingers on my pulse.

'I'd die without you,' I managed to say. I began to laugh, and turned silent in the middle of my laughter, listening appalled to the false merriment of my noisy voice. I put my hands on her cheeks, her cheeks were cold like ice.

'It's you, really you,' I breathed. 'Terry, don't you know me, this is Hugh! Terry! Terry!'

Her cheeks were cold like ice. She collapsed into my arms. I took off her clothes and put her to bed. She was asleep before I covered her with blankets. I sat by the hammock, staring at her, putting out my hand to touch her. I grew sick as I thought of the death in life that would be my portion, lacking her. All the air in the world was too little for the gusty suspiration of my panic breath. Fear's constricting fingers gripped me in their hold. She wakened once, roused by my presence beside her; she said in a gentle voice, 'I was sleeping, Hugh.' She smiled and said, 'Aren't you coming to bed, Hugh? You look tired.'

WE STAYED AWAKE throughout the day on the Twelfth. Only our ears' expectancy kept us from falling asleep. It was a warm drowsy day; the heat of the yellowing sun, the sound of bumble-bees, the smell of heather in flower, lulled us and drugged our senses half to sleep save our ears that harkened through the hours for sounds that did not come.

'The first day of autumn,' Terry breathed, interrupting a long silence.

'The last day of summer,' I returned.

'Och, no,' she said, 'summer will have plenty of last days yet. We've had rare luck in the weather, Hugh.'

'We couldn't have managed if the year was wet,' I agreed.

'It's too dry now. The hill's like tinder. A spark would put it in a blaze. We must be careful with the ashes, Terry. This would be a hot corner if the rank heather round about caught fire.'

We looked involuntarily to the east where we had seen heavy smoke rising in the past few days, as if from a forest fire in the region of Rothiemurchus.

'It couldn't have been woods on fire,' I said, reverting to an oft-discussed topic. 'Or it would have been burning still.'

'The smoke has vanished,' Terry agreed. 'There might have been rain there though we had none.'

I shook my head.

'Not with these blue skies,' I told her. 'If it doesn't rain soon I needn't bother going out to stalk. Even as it is I can scarcely come near stags for the noise of the moss crackling under my feet.'

In the late afternoon Terry voiced our mutual thought.

'I haven't heard a single shot,' she said.

'Not one,' I concurred.

'I've been waiting all day ready to be angry,' she confessed with a smile.

'Angry?' I asked.

'If I heard shooting, I'd be angry to think men should go out for sport, at such a time.'

'They went out to kill grouse in the last war,' I informed her.

'Did they? Hadn't they plenty of killing?'

'I'm not sure but that I'd prefer to hear the guns blattering to-day,' I went on. 'Things must be bad, Terry. I never heard a Twelfth like this before. Nor any one else. It'd be better to hear the guns—if we knew they were shooting grouse.'

'We know things are bad,' she told me. 'Duncan said—'

'He didn't say much,' I interrupted.

'Not with his tongue, Hugh.'

'It's a wonder we haven't seen any one,' she continued. 'If the country is full of deserters and stragglers—'

'He warned us,' I put in.

'And soldiers rounding them up—' she added.

I rose to my feet and stretched myself.

'He could have told us much more than he did,' she said. 'He was saving us, hiding the worst from us—where are you going, Hugh?'

'To kill a grouse, Terry,' I answered. 'We've always had a grouse on the Twelfth.'

She jumped up beside me and caught my arm.

'Don't go, Hugh,' she begged earnestly. 'Please don't go! maybe it's a bad sign for human folk, this quiet Twelfth, but men's misfortune has this much good in it, that it makes a truce for the poor birds of the country. Hugh, there'll be other times when we're more needing food. We'll let this Twelfth be a holiday from killing.'

'We used to reckon that we could use the new potatoes from the field by the Twelfth of August,' I said, sitting down again.

'Don't make my mouth water,' she reproached me. 'I've been longing for new potatoes—'

'With milk and fresh butter,' I suggested.

'Why are you tempting me!' she cried.

Next day, in the evening, I took Duncan's rifle and slipped a handful of cartridges into my pocket.

'Where are you going, Hugh?' Terry demanded. 'Why are you taking that rifle? Won't it make a loud noise?'

'I'm leaving the .22 with you,' I answered, 'in case a grouse comes near while I'm away. Don't sit up for me, Terry, it may be morning before I come back.'

'Can't I come?' she begged. 'I'll not be a nuisance. I won't be tired or in the way—listen!'

She tiptoed through a brake of long heather.

'You didn't hear that, did you?' she asked triumphantly. 'The deer won't take fright from *my* step, I'll walk so lightly. I'll tread as soft as a mouse.'

I could not help laughing at her sober face.

'Another time,' I put her off.

'Why not this time?' she demanded. 'I know,' she went on, 'you're not going after a deer at all, Hugh. You're planning something and you don't want to tell me.'

'What would I be planning?' I cried. 'Now, where's Duncan's game-bag—have you a bite of food I can take in my pocket in case I'm hindered? Are you angry, Terry? Won't you say good hunting?'

'No,' she answered flatly. 'Take care of yourself and come safe home,' she whispered a moment afterwards. 'Don't let any harm come to you. I'll be waiting for you.'

I went down into the gully and spied the country to the south, making a great show of looking for beasts for Terry's benefit. When I had assured myself that there were no deer to be seen from where she stood beside the cave I walked up the defile towards Ardverikie Forest. As soon as I was out of sight of the cave I slackened my pace. Darkness was still some hours off, and the evening was too bright for my project. I settled myself behind a stone and smoked a precious pipeful of tobacco that I had gleaned from the corners of my jacket's pockets, and while I waited for night I amused myself by taking imaginary snapshots at boulders. I had often used Duncan's rifle in the old days when he took me with him to kill a hind. It came naturally to my hands now. It was far superior to my own .303, and I had brought down a beast at three hundred yards with it, more than once.

At length when it seemed dark enough to proceed I loaded the rifle carefully, filling the magazine with seven shells and leaving the breach empty. In this way I could carry it in perfect security with the safety catch off and yet load and be ready in a twinkling. I swung from my first course, bending more westerly towards the shining goal of Loch Laggan.

It was very dark by the time I reached the woods along the River Pattock and I regretted that I had not taken the risk of going ahead while daylight lasted. I blundered through the thick scrubby outskirts of the wood. Tussocks and open drains tripped me up, I went to the knees in scummy pools. I have never recovered from the horror of that time when I was nearly drowned in a bog in the Durc, and I dragged myself trembling from these sloughs as if they harboured venomous reptiles. Branches struck my face or caught my clothes as I passed. I fell a hundred times, and the rifle, swinging over my shoulder, belaboured my head with its butt as I scrambled to my feet. I could not afford a hand to hold the rifle since both hands were needed to warn me of obstacles and ward off the trees I would have run against had I not kept my hands outstretched before me. I knew that I had a deer fence to cross before I arrived at the Pattock. I walked with groping hands outstretched for a good half-mile before I came to the fence, and when I did reach it I came unawares against it and hurt my arm.

I was exasperated and nervous. When an owl left its perch in the branches above my head with a soft *Whoof* of feathers I had the rifle in my hands and loaded and cocked and pointed forward in one frenzied movement. I could hear the river brawling ahead of me, my only guide through the mirk. I headed for the noise, fearing to miss the shallow upper part of the stream where it could be forded. I began to fancy that

I had kept too low, and that each step forward was going to precipitate me over the edge of the cliffs which guard the lower course of the river.

The stream was very small. Its waters felt warm even to my hot touch. I bathed my wrists and my forehead before I crossed into the main forest. I found the path leading to Gallovie, between the river and the fir woods, and followed it as best I could. The Pattock, ending its broad shallow course, plunged into a chasm; on my left hand I had the dark windless wood, on my right a sheer descent from the verge of my path into the river's pools and cascades. It was pitch dark and very hot. Sweat ran down my face, blinding me more effectually than the dark night. I began to start like a nervous animal. I fancied the trees were keeping step with me, or dangerous creatures hid in the depth of the forest walked abreast with me. The dark wood repelled me and I found myself walking on the brink of the cliff. I veered from that danger until I ran into the trees where the path curved, and I sprang away in fear.

I had gone about half a mile down the path when a sudden thrashing noise, accompanied by the sound of harsh choked breathing, brought me to a fearful standstill. The noise was directly in my way, I could not go ahead without approaching it. I forced my limbs to carry me off the path, into the wood. As soon as I left the path and halted in the shade of the wood, if shadow it could be called which was but more intensely dark, everything fell silent again; I could hear the river but no other sound. I brought the rifle from my shoulder to assure myself with shaking hands that it was ready. I waited what seemed a great length of time before I ventured to move, keeping within the wood, off the path. When I had travelled twenty steps the noise broke out once more with renewed force; I was near enough to the edge of the wood to see the narrow strip of sky between the trees on both sides of the river. I saw a monstrous form uprear itself against the lesser darkness of the sky; it rose to the height of the trees, a few yards from me, and fell, and rose again. The choking sound repeated itself more loudly. I

was shaking so that I could scarcely keep my fingers on
the safety catch and the trigger of my rifle. I levelled the
rifle at the patch of blank darkness from which the shape
had risen as I waited. I began to hear a low sobbing noise,
like the drawing in of difficult breath, that the water's voice
had drowned until this moment. I trailed my feet closer to
the thing, with infinite caution, ready to retreat. My eyes
caught a glimpse of a tree-top which seemed to bend and
shake, moving alone amongst its motionless fellows. As I
stared at the bending plumes of that tree the Thing leapt
up again, and I saw horns outlined against the vague sky.
I turned back the safety catch of my rifle, and commenced
to laugh. I could hear the hysterical note of my laughter.
I scolded myself aloud saying, 'Shut up! shut up! shut
up!' And then, 'Frightened to death by a stag in a snare!'

I was near enough, now that I knew what I was looking
for, to make out the shape of the stag that hung suspended
by its head, or horns, from a young tree beside the path.
I ventured closer. Immediately the brute began to plunge
and rear. Flying hooves missed my face by an inch. I felt
the wind of the fore-feet as they lashed out; the skin of
my neck was prickling and my spine felt cold. Those sharp
hooves would have cut my face to ribbons if I had been a
step nearer. The horrible shuddering of the poor creature's
breath started again.

'The damn fools!' I raged aloud, 'to hang their snare
too low and leave the brute in agony.'

I was so angry that I forgot to be wary. The stag's pain
could scarcely be listened to. I took my handkerchief and
bound my sheath-knife to the muzzle of the rifle like a
bayonet. When the deer ceased to struggle and hung quietly
I guessed for its heart and drove the weapon with all my
strength at the vague bulk. I drew back as fast as I could
recover from the thrust. The beast reared itself for the
last time. It was a lucky stroke. The random blade had
pierced a vital place. The sweeping horns loomed over
me with the sky behind them; the deer uttered a sound
between groan and cough. Frothy blood shaken from its

nostrils in the final convulsion fell on my face. The stag
fell, dragging the tree-top into a great bow as the dead
weight came on it. When I was sure the beast was dead
I loosened the wire from its neck and cut off its head and
flung it in the river. I gralloched the carcass and rolled the
forequarters after the head and hid the haunches on a bluff
that I could not mistake, to await my return. I was glad
to have venison so easily although the brute's cruel death
troubled my mind. I consoled myself with the thought that
I had punished whoever set the snare. I could fancy the
poacher's anger, and I told myself, 'Serve him right,' yet the
stag's breath was still in my ears. I felt implicated in needless
brutality. I went ahead towards Gallovie more rapidly than
I had travelled heretofore. Anger ousted fear and made my
previous caution seem cowardly. As I walked a new thought
struck me. It was very strange that a poacher should dare
to set a trap for deer on this path of all places. Stalkers
used the path daily, fishers and sightseers frequented it.
I recalled the silence of the Twelfth and what Duncan let
slip about famished bands of stragglers roving the country.
I thought of Terry with sudden panic. I began to run as
fast as my legs would carry me, down the path, out of the
wood, into the meadows of Inverpattock. The normal past
is still the background to my thoughts. Perhaps there are no
stalkers now, no fishers by the Pattock, no sightseers save
the sightless wide-eyed dead.

The path, leaving the forest, brought me to a cooler lighter
world where my panic abated as quickly as it rose. My own
experience in the plantation beyond the river was enough
to teach me that strangers, inexpert in the country, would
never come on our cave by night. I was ready to reproach
myself for a timorous imaginative fool by the time I came
to the foot-bridges that span the Pattock's divided streams.
I sat down on the rail of one bridge to draw my breath.
The country seemed lost in sleep. Every house was dark.
I guessed it was past one in the morning. The blurred
valley sloped upwards into woods, and the woods ended
in a jet-black line against the hills, and the hills climbed

against the sky. I felt a touch of frost in the air. The deep
blue of the sky lightened towards the north, as I had often
seen in frosty weather when the wild fires of frost that burn
around the pole irradiate the Monadhliah scarp, warning us
of winter. A sliver of white moon, hung like a sword in blue
air, rested over Gallovie. I went into the fields to steal the
new potatoes I had come for.

I came first on a field of corn. It was trampled down
as if by a herd of cattle. When I kneeled to peer at the
ground I could distinguish the mark of boots, and cattle's
hooves, in the soft earth. I crossed from that field into
its neighbour. It was drilled as if for potatoes or turnips
but nothing grew from the drills. I kneeled once more to
assure myself that my eyes were not deceiving me. The
night was too peaceful and normal for such discoveries as
affronted my senses. Half-withered green shaws lay between
the drills, with yellowed turnip tops and potatoes the size of a
marble. I commenced to delve hurriedly in the tattered drills,
groping in the earth with my fingers for potatoes overlooked
by whoever had forestalled me. I found a few potatoes, but
when I had scraped and scratched methodically for half an
hour, gleaning no more than a few pounds of tiny potatoes,
I tried a new plan. I walked up and down the drills in
search of crops that had escaped the harvesters. I found
a crop here and there hidden amongst shaws. At length
I had a fair weight in my bag. I left the potato patch
to hunt for turnips. They likewise had been uprooted by
hasty inexpert hands. I gathered a dozen bulbs which had
been overlooked. Then I stuffed the game-bag with green
turnip-tops until it would hold no more and I was ready to
go home.

I crossed the bridge. The climbing moon, and my accus-
tomed eyes, made my path plain, but my eyes kept turning
towards Gallovie. I was devoured with curiosity which would
not be gainsaid. I walked a few steps on my homeward path,
and halted.

'It won't be dawn for a good two hours,' I told myself. I
hid my game-bag under the bridge and, rifle in hand, went

to spy round Gallovie. I had no idea what I wanted to find. A fever of curiosity spurred me.

There is often a wind before dawn after windless nights. Such a breath began to stir now amongst the trees, and in the summer-parched grass. I heard it over the woods long before it reached me. While it was still and calm where I stood I heard the sighing in the tree-tops which presaged a breeze; a door banged in the cluster of buildings. I tiptoed up the hill against the cooling breeze. The door banged again. There was no other sound or sign of life amongst the houses and farm buildings. I trod so warily that I could hear the beating of my heart louder by far than my cautious step. But it was dark underfoot and I trod twice on dead branches which snapped with a noise like a rifle, or so it seemed to my ears. I froze at the sound; I dared not turn the safety catch of my rifle in case it was heard; I kept my thumb on the catch and my forefinger on the trigger.

I could hear no noise of cattle or horses. If they were not in the steading they should be in the meadows. I gazed every way and saw no beast. I heard nothing but the wind and the river and my tumultuous blood. I reached a fence. Walking alongside it with one hand on the top wire to guide me, I came to a gateway. An iron gate was lying flat on the ground, torn from its hinges. I stepped across it, marking its place lest I required to retreat hastily. I entered the courtyard. The doors of the steading were open. The doorways yawned black in the wall. I went cautiously from one door to another. Some of the doors were gone, others had broken panels and their locks were torn out. The place had the aspect of desolation. I was afraid to strike a match or go inside the byres and stables. It occurred to me again that I had not heard a dog barking. I ventured as far as the kennels. Their iron doors were open, their occupants mute, or gone. I crept back until I came to a cottar house. Its door was shut, but I could see it was not properly closed. It leaned from inside against its frame, without hinges or lock. The window-panes were broken in every window, the garden like our own trampled with many feet; I found potato shaws scattered on the ground amongst a litter of broken glass and charred clothes and broken dishes. A fire had been lighted in a corner of the garden. I found hinges amongst its embers. Bits of painted wood lay half-burnt around. As I went out of that garden a breath of abominable air met me, a stench of decaying flesh such as I had often felt when I passed near the rotting maggot-infested carcass of a deer on the hill in midsummer. The smell came the more abominably upon the night's sweet air; I felt my gorge rising, I ran with my hand to my mouth until I was near the river. A mouthful of bile spewed itself into my hand against the strength of my clenched jaws.

The sky was lightening in the east. I hurried to be gone before day surprised me in strange country. I carried the stag's haunches out of the wood and as far as I was able to bring them into the hills. I hid them securely to await my return. The sun came up to lighten my way home obliterating the fears of night. Terry had a fire burning.

'I thought you'd never come,' she said. 'What have you in the bag, Hugh? You didn't get a stag after all. You're all blood! Your face is all blood! Hugh! where were you?'

I spilled the bag's contents on the floor.

'New potatoes!' she cried, 'and turnips! Oh, Hugh! But where did you get them? Sit down and I'll take off your boots. They're soaking—'

I told her part of the night's affairs while she gave me dry clothes and set out food for me.

'I can't eat them,' she said, looking at the potatoes with distaste. 'Think of the risk you ran—it wasn't worth it—if anything happened to you—'

'Risk?' I returned. 'I don't think there was any. I don't think there's a soul save ourselves left alive in this country.'

I kept some things secret even from her. The smell of death, rank and hideous, was in my nostrils as I spoke, and ate, and tried to sleep. I shuddered when I let my thoughts go back and I smelled again that foul air I breathed. She brought me dry clothes, making pretence that she believed it was cold which made my blood congeal.

WE HAVE BEEN very idle these past few days. Our firewood is home, the cave is snug against winter, there is nothing for us to do save sleep all night and lie in the sun all day.

Time goes faster here than ever it did while we lived in our house. We can scarcely believe it is mid-autumn already, though winter looks down on us each morning from peaks dusted with new snow. Midday's fervour dissolves the snow, yet the time seems the more autumnal for the brief fierce heat of the sun.

It is autumn indeed. The bloom of the heather is withered brown. Cock grouse waken us with their calling from dun hillocks, and I am sure I heard a stag roar yesterday.

'A fortnight too early,' I told Terry. 'It brings winter on us with a rush.'

'I didn't hear it,' she answered. 'I've heard that roe-deer barking, though. We'll be right in the middle of the stags here when they start roaring in earnest.'

'Oh you'll hear a chorus all right,' I assured her. 'Enough to frighten you on frosty nights—'

The light of the sun is no longer rich and mellow as it was a month ago. The sun shines with a thin white heat. We feel the heat of noon far more than we did in July, perhaps because the nights are growing cold. We wakened shivering one night last week. When I rose to fetch deer-skin rugs I looked out at the door of the cave to see the night. It was so lovely I began to call Terry, telling her to hurry as if the silver moon and frost-bespangled earth were too beautiful to remain. The moon was full in an empty sky. The world it lightened had no colours save the white light of the moon and shadows as black as jet. The large moon, lifted in vacancy, gave me a strange feeling of the round earth itself, sailing in space upon its voyage, with us its infinitesimal cargo. The world had valleys as the moon; I saw the valleys of the moon, and under them our country with its hills.

The leaves of the birch wood are bright yellow. Rowan trees with scarlet fruit amongst their crimson, brown, and black leaves stand in the golden setting of the birches. The bent grass of the forest is tawny yellow.

We have made our cave tight and snug. The floor is covered with deer-skins. Every chink and cranny in the gable is stopped with clay. We have a double door of skins and canvas to exclude storm.

'We've one thing to be thankful for,' I told Terry when the new snow appeared. 'We are under the snow-line; I've been watching the clouds on dirty days. We lie just under them. All we get of them is flying scuds of mist. It'll make a big difference in midwinter. If we were above the snow-line we'd have rain and sleet and snow practically without cease.'

'A pretty prospect,' she said laughing. 'Oh, Hugh! I wish you could see yourself.'

'What's the matter with me?' I demanded.

'You're not brown, you're black,' she cried. 'If ever I saw a gipsy—I really must set to and mend your clothes,' she added more seriously.

'You've a wild look about yourself, Terry. That tangled black mop of yours—Do I look a ruffian?' I asked ruefully, examining my arms and legs. I was wearing shorts and boots without stockings and the sleeves of my shirt were cut away. My arms and legs were burnt with the sun. Terry had on her shortest skirt. She also was without stockings and her blouse lacked sleeves. Her head was bare. Her hair over her forehead was bleached with the sun.

'I'm going to wear rags while I can,' I continued. 'Pretty soon we'll have to put on winter clothes again.'

'Yes,' she agreed, and sighed. 'I'm loath to think that summer's nearly spent.'

'Och, winter won't be so deathly bad,' I told her. 'There'll be fine days. I don't mind a storm really, Terry. It's fun to hear the wind battering at a door you know it can't break down—when you've good food and plenty of firewood.'

'Many a one won't have that,' she said gravely. 'What will winter bring for the rest of the world?'

'I've stopped grieving myself for others' woe,' I answered slowly. 'We require all our time to take thought for ourselves, Terry.'

'You know you don't mean that,' she said. 'The worse our own lot, the more we think of others.'

'Then let them do as we did,' I cried impatiently, 'let them fend for themselves. I'm not going to waste the last fine days of the year pondering about the hypothetical woes of the world.'

'You never told me all that happened on the journey you made to Gallovie,' she accused.

'What!' I cried, startled; 'yes, I did, Terry, I told you every single thing.'

Her eyes showed her incredulity but she did not say more.

We spent a good deal of time carrying home fir roots from the head of Loch Coulter. The waves and floods of many years had fretted away the moss by the water-side. When the loch subsided in summer a jumble of roots was laid bare and quickly dried. We often marvelled at these roots. They grew so thickly that their branches were interlocked and we had to cut them adrift from each other with the axe. In the days when the forest grew of which these roots were a token no one could possibly have traversed this country, for the trees must have grown so close together that to pass between them was impossible. But not only were the roots close together and interwoven, they ranked three layers deep, as if three successive forests had grown and died in the moss. Yet no modern trees will thrive in moss, far less flourish and grow to the size that the roots of those old trees indicated. We found roots, weathered and broken, but still three or four feet in diameter, and what we found was not the whole root but only the heart, the resinous pith, of ancient giants.

The fir was too resinous to be used freely on our fire. We lighted the fire, when the peat was slow to burn up from its ashes in the morning, with slivers of fir; once Terry threw on a sizable piece; it exploded into flame with a yellow blaze that filled the chimney and ascended clear of the chimney can into the open air, a beacon that would attract attention from miles away.

It was easy to gather the fir, but fetching it uphill to the cave proved a slow monotonous labour. We hid our store of kindling near the cave under slabs of stone.

We had our sticks in safety and our cave prepared for bad weather by the last week of August. We took energy from the sun, and after an evening and a morning spent trailing roots uphill we were still ready to go afield for rowans and cranberries and averans. We ventured once as far as the Truim to poach salmon in a pool I knew. I caught a fish with my hands. We crossed the railway. The rails were red with rust as if they had been long disused.

'They soon grow rusty. A couple of days without traffic will do it,' I said.

'Surely not in this dry weather,' Terry said.

'There's always dew at night,' I assured her.

We had no doubt in our minds. Catastrophe had arrived on our country. We did but argue about the things we saw to save ourselves from relating them together, from thinking of their cause.

We were too greedy to let the salmon lie in cure. But we split trout and pike open and sprinkled them with salt and laid them out in the sun; in a few days they were kippered, ready to hang in the cave beside our fire.

WE WAKENED EARLY on the morning of the 10th with the feeling that something uncommon had disturbed us. I opened my eyes to find Terry sitting bolt upright in the hammock beside me.

'What was that?' she demanded. 'Did you hear anything, Hugh?'

'I thought I did,' I answered.

I had scarcely spoken when the noise that roused us repeated itself.

'What noise is that?' Terry whispered.

'Guns,' I said.

'Guns! then they *are* shooting grouse somewhere.'

'Not with rifles,' I told her grimly.

'I didn't know it was rifles, Hugh,' she said in a constrained voice and became silent. I began to fling off the bedclothes.

'Where are you going, Hugh?' Terry asked in the same forced voice.

'To put on my clothes.'

'Hugh—' She caught my arm and clung to it. She was still sitting upright. I could sense her rigid expectancy though I could not see her features in the dim light of the cave.

'I'll cook breakfast,' I told her gently, laying my free hand on the hand that gripped me to disengage it. Her fingers clutched me, resisting my efforts to loosen them.

'Let me go, honey,' I said. 'Lie down and wrap yourself in the blankets. It must be frosty—there's a keen air—'

'Are there deer-forests over there?' she asked, ignoring my words. 'Would they be shooting deer? Hugh! speak to me! is it deer they'd be shooting?'

115

'Not with volleys,' I said, laying aside pretence.

'Volleys!' Her voice rose and she cried, 'Hugh! Hugh! don't leave me! stay with me, I'm frightened.'

'There! there!' I said, going back beside her and taking her in my arms. 'Don't you be frightened, honey, I'm with you, nothing can hurt you.'

Her rigid form collapsed against me.

'I'm frightened!' she muttered.

'Hush, Terry,' I whispered. 'Lie down and keep yourself warm and comfortable while I make breakfast.'

'I can't help it!' she exclaimed, shaking herself free of my hold. 'I know something dreadful's happening—'

The sound of a ragged volley, amongst the hills to the south, interrupted her.

'That noise!' she cried, covering her ears with her hands.

'It's a great long way off,' I said.

'It's nearer and nearer every day,' she went on drearily. 'I can feel it coming nearer. Like an avalanche, slowly, slowly moving—'

'But we're safe here, no harm can touch us. Who'd come here?' I broke in.

'Falling to crush us!' she went on as if I had not spoken. 'Oh God, my heart!'

'Terry!' I scolded, 'you mustn't take on like this, it's not right. We should be thankful we are safe.'

'Safe! Sometimes I think we should have stayed. We might have been able to help—'

'Lie down and keep yourself warm,' I besought her, 'and that'll help me. You're chittering with cold. I don't want to have an invalid on my hands.'

'Yes, I'm cold,' she whispered like a submissive child. 'I'm terribly cold. Feel my hands, Hugh, they're like ice. You're very kind to me, Hugh,' she murmured as I tucked her in. 'Very good to me,' her voice continued faintly. 'I'm sleepy, Hugh.'

We have heard no more firing since then. In the silence of night before we sleep, and when we start awake through the long dark hours, our imagination hears the deadly sound, nearer, dangerous, loud above the rising winds of autumn. There is very little work for us to do nowadays. We sit, pretending for each other's sake that we have no deeper thought in our heads than pleasure in the sun. Our pretence is thin. It hides nothing from ourselves. Once or twice of late it has failed. Last night we wakened together and I knew, without requiring to see or hear her, that Terry was not asleep.

'I can't sleep,' I said.

'I can't sleep, either,' she repeated simply.

'It must have been the cold that wakened us,' I went on. 'Would you like more clothes on the bed, Terry?'

'How far away was that noise?' she asked, ignoring my question.

'Beyond Benalder,' I told her.

'Very near,' she whispered.

'Far enough to be safe for us,' I returned.

'Safe!' Her voice fell. 'We can't pretend for ever,' she said wearily. 'It's come to us and we can't escape knowing that it's come. The trains, our house, Duncan, Gallovie—'

'We've got to go the way we must,' I whispered. 'There's you and me still—'

'All alone now, Hugh. Oh, Hugh, don't ever leave me! It's nothing to die, if you're with me. It was silly of me to be frightened—when I heard—the guns. I'm not frightened of anything when you're near me. How warm you are!'

My flesh began to grue and I clenched my teeth to keep them from chattering. Out of vague and dispersed trifles, out of rumours and hints and Duncan's scanty words, a close and deadly menace raised itself, taking shape and form at the sound of Terry's terror-stricken voice renouncing fear. I put up my hand to the rock above my head. This rock that pressed down over us, these cliffs that lowered to close us in, assumed the aspect of a portent, and danger, implicit in our way of life, caged us in.

IN A FEW DAYS after that morning when we were wakened
by the sound of rifle-fire rain came on with boisterous winds.
Now in the general uproar our straining ears could no longer
distinguish separate and ambiguous noises, nor constrain
each far-off murmur to the likeness of guns beyond the
hills. Our ears could not forebode danger while they were
deafened with rushing winds and the tumult of waters; our
minds, which had been oppressed with the fear of danger
coming daily nearer, became calm as the weather rose to
wilder storms.

We had been silent in our cave, and preoccupied. The
realization of what we craved yet dreaded to know had thrust
itself upon us. We saw that as our knowledge increased, so
did that which we had fled to avoid come inexorably on, and
our calm sunlit haven, untrod and soundless save for late bees
and grouse and the roaring stags, assumed the appearance
of an arena round which the rage of the world gathered.
We were helpless before this thing that stalked into our
knowledge, into our hearing, into our sight. Because our
imagination could create only vague pictures of what was
happening from what we saw and heard, our peril was the
vaster. We could conceive of nothing but general ruin to
explain the ruin of our garden and Gallovie's fate. Duncan's
careful warning filled the land with famished troops of
desperate men whose strife and clash we heard when that
dawn brought the sound of guns.

But as the weather changed, so did our spirits. There was
exultation in the wind; rain drove in slanting sheets, the
wind amongst the cliffs over our heads was like the surf of the
ocean. We were warm and dry in our cave. We sat inside the

door, watching the squalls scud down the gully and spread themselves over the moor, over the valley, until they blotted out Speyside. Loch Coulter was white with foam. Whirling gouts of spray rose from the loch, and the wind carried them away, to drench the moor and flood the Spey and lace the seldom-seen Monadhliahs with silver streams. Floods that fell from the lip of the precipices around us were caught by the wind, blown into mist by the wind, flung back on the hills that gathered them from the clouds.

It grew cold and the land was a vast bog save where the black streaming cliffs rose to touch the racing sky. Our cave was warm and dry. Even when the clouds were riven momently from the peaks and we saw new snow, not the white powdery coat of the year's first snow, but leaden stuff under the leaden sky, we were not downcast.

We ate, we slept, we watched the days scud past. We seemed to lose track of everything. Our larder was almost empty but I shot grouse from the door of the cave, and we lived on them from day to day, from hand to mouth. Terry unravelled a pair of my stockings to reknit them. I busied myself cleaning the rifles. We piled on fire and prided ourselves on our comfort.

The weather began to clear yesterday. After midday the rain ended and I called Terry to view a break in the western sky. By night the sky was empty. The wind blew as strongly as ever though the sun shone without clouds. Night comes down early now. It hid the world, save where a snowy peak glimmered. We heard the hoarse voice of many streams. Lying awake we listened in silence to their shouting. When we wakened in the morning the wind was down. It was very cold; the burns though noisy yet were falling and we surveyed a bare swept country, prepared for winter. The sun commenced to warm the morning air. The light of morning was very clear; we could see the most remote distance as if nothing interposed between ourselves and it save space. The Cairngorms made miniatures of themselves upon the horizon, against the green-blue sky.

'Autumn's done,' I told Terry.

She looked into the vacant sky. The clouds, the gulls, the traitorous peewits, all were gone together, swept away by the wind. The birds that had left us made so great a lack, we felt as if all the birds of the air had gone. Stags were roaring in the corries; their throats like the brawling streams did not break the silence that we listened to, nor convince us that our empty country was peopled, but rather they made a background for silence.

The day grew warm. We sat outside the cave to enjoy the sun. The birches were bare, their drab yellow leaves carpeted the ground; the rowan trees had lost their leaves. But here and there in the smoky woods we saw a leafless tree hung with scarlet berries, daring winter. A cloud of small birds swept along the ground beside us, and into the air like leaves in a whirling wind. They fell, and rose, all in one flock, and settled for a moment amongst the birches under our cave, above the loch.

'Autumn's done,' I said again. 'I must get a beast tomorrow. Pretty soon the stags will be too lean to eat.'

'It's warm still,' Terry said. 'There's heat in the sun. If it holds like this to-morrow couldn't we do something, Hugh? Couldn't we have a picnic?'

'The ground's as wet as muck,' I reminded her.

'Och, then we mustn't sit on the ground. It's the last chance of the year, Hugh. We were always having picnics in the old days—'

'I'd like to bathe once more in Loch Coulter, before winter comes,' I confessed.

'Won't it be dreadfully cold?' she asked, shivering.

'No,' I answered, 'with all the rain there's been the loch will be as warm as milk. What'll we have to eat, Terry?'

'I hope it's a day like this,' she said; and then, 'When will the birds come back again, Hugh?'

AS WE WENT down and came near Loch Coulter, Terry said, 'When shall we bathe again, Hugh?'

'Mebbe in March,' I told her. 'It can be hot in March.'

'We must begin to think about next year,' she went on slowly.

'What are we going to think about next year?' I demanded.

'We can't live for ever on our stores, Hugh.'

'Well?' I inquired roughly.

'Don't be angry with me to-day, Hugh,' she pleaded.

'I'm sorry,' I said. 'I didn't mean to sound angry. Oh, it's always the same, when we mean to spend one day just being happy worries come crowding on us—'

'I didn't mean to worry you, Hugh,' she whispered. 'Och, never heed next year—'

'We must heed it,' I said.

'Not to-day,' she replied, 'another day, Hugh, but not to-day.'

'To-day and every day. There's not a moment of our time will ever be free again. To-morrow's food, every day's danger—where will it end?'

I looked drearily across the blue waters of the loch. I felt her hand touch mine timidly.

'Don't pay any attention to me,' I bade her.

'I think we'll catch one of the goats that are running wild on the Farrow,' she said with forced cheerfulness. 'Like Robinson Crusoe, you know. Can't you make rennet for cheese from the stomachs of young rabbits, Hugh?'

'Yes, or lambs while they're very young, or deer calves, or any beast while it's being suckled by its mother.'

'There you are!' she continued. 'We'll have milk and cheese and white, white butter. Then we'll dig a bit of ground and plant potatoes—'

'Where is the seed coming from?' I asked ironically.

'Couldn't we get potatoes and lots of things from—from round about?'

'Where?' I cried. 'Oh, there's an easier way, the way we'll go.'

'What way is that, Hugh?' she asked.

'The way of our fathers, raiding and stealing, thieving like our ancestors.'

'It'd be better for us to die, Hugh.'

'That's easy too.'

'Hugh!' she cried. 'Why are you like this to-day?'

'I don't know, Terry. Oh Christ, I can't see, it's dark and hopeless every way I turn.'

'We'll go out to the hill for meat to-morrow,' she said simply. 'I think it'll do us good. We've been too idle lately, Hugh. I often notice,' she went on in earnest tones, 'we get like this, downcast and hopeless, when we have nothing to occupy us. You are always happier after a hard day on the hill, Hugh.'

'What's the benefit of feeling better for a few hours when it's worse afterwards?' I exclaimed.

'That's nonsense, Hugh, and besides, we need meat. What are you seeing?' she asked sharply.

'Sheep,' I answered. 'We can eat mutton now, Terry, and have tallow candles to light us, and skins to keep us warm.'

'We're not sheep-stealers yet, Hugh,' she said.

'There's no stealing when there's no owner,' I replied.

'No owner! What do you mean?'

'Why are the sheep still here, all scattered everyway, and their lambs with them that should have been weaned and sold six weeks ago? Have you seen a shepherd, or heard his dogs? Why is there wool in tufts on every low branch of this wood? If there were owners still, would the sheep be out here now, with their lambs, and some not even clipped?'

'I don't know,' she whispered.

'Why should we try to blind ourselves—the worst we imagined isn't so bad as the things that have happened there! there! there!' I spread my arms wildly to the places beyond our country where men used to live.

She began to take off her clothes and wade into the loch. I followed her. Winter had couriers in the viewless air. We hurried, breathless with cold, out of the water to dry ourselves.

'There's frost in that wind,' I told her. As I rubbed myself dry my skin began to tingle and my flesh to glow. I started to run up and down the sandy foreshore of the bay where we swam. I pounded the firm sand with my feet and felt wisps of sand rise between my toes. Terry stood on the bank laughing at my antics. She shook her tangled hair over her eyes and began to comb it aside with her fingers. As I turned from watching her to raise my arms to the pale sun I caught a glimpse of moving figures in the gorge beneath our cave.

'Down, Terry! down!' I whispered fiercely, flinging myself flat on the sand as I spoke.

'What's the matter, Hugh?' she asked in bewilderment, looking about her without obeying my command.

'For God's sake lie down or you'll destroy us both,' I muttered furiously. I began to worm my way to the place where she crouched with her head in the air and a petulant look on her face.

'Keep your damned head down,' I bade her with increasing anger. I was now beside her. I commenced to gather my clothes in my arms.

'Get your clothes together,' I whispered. 'For the love of God do as I bid you, Terry.'

Her cheeks grew white and without another word, without even a murmur of complaint, she followed me as I crawled uphill to the shelter of the wood. Sharp stones struck our bare limbs, heather and branches scratched us, we were wet and filthy and cold with the muck of bogs we crossed. I could scarcely keep my teeth from chattering and I heard Terry's breath come and go in painful sighs.

'Not far now,' I encouraged her hoarsely. She followed me in dogged silence.

'Put on your stockings and shoes first,' I bade her when we reached the thicket I had aimed for. 'If we've to run we must be shod. Put on your clothes as fast as you can—I'll steal a look—'

She sat down obediently on a lichen-covered stone and began to clothe herself. There were long deep scratches on her legs.

'Here,' I said, giving her my handkerchief, 'put that under your stocking. It'll keep it from sticking to you if there's blood when you grow warm again.'

She took the handkerchief without a word. I dragged my clothes on; they were sopping and made me feel colder than when I was naked. My left knee was aching with a knock I had taken on a stone. Terry looked at me with a grey anxious face, I tried to smile.

'I think it's all right now,' I whispered, and left her and skulked down from tree to tree until I came into a glade that opened on the gorge. I saw about a dozen men, with four or five dogs at their heels, advancing in the direction of the loch. I did not wait to see more. Immediately I perceived the rifles on their backs, and the crew's wild air, I slipped back to where Terry cowered. She stood up at my approach, gazing at me with enormous eyes. Her hands, blue with cold, went to her breast.

'Oh! Oh!' she said, articulating with difficulty. 'I didn't see you coming! you frightened me!'

'We must get back to the cave,' I whispered, 'there may be other men—'

'Are there men?' she asked in low tones.

I nodded.

'If they find the cave we are as good as dead,' I went on. 'What a fool I was to leave the rifle!'

We climbed up the hill-side as far as the wood gave us shelter. Then, casting back and fore, we ranged the steep until we found a ravine gouged out by a winter-flooding burn. Though the course of the stream was dry there were pools of water in rocky pots in the gully. We could not avoid them. We trailed ourselves up the gorge, splattering through the pools, clambering up dry falls of rock and shale-slides with infinite care lest we dislodged a stone and sent it tumbling down to warn the men below. Now and then as I crawled I could see them beneath us if I raised my head so much as an inch. They seemed very near; I could scarcely believe they had not our progress in plain view.

At length we lay breathless on the summit almost directly above our cave. I crept to the edge of the cliff whence I could peer at the disturbers of our peace. They were making north along the shore of Loch Coulter. Their dogs stalked at their heels. We waited until the company of men and dogs vanished over the rim of moor beyond the loch. No other danger showed itself. We searched the country, especially the valley to the west from which these men had come. We saw nothing there to alarm us.

'Are they gone, Hugh?' Terry whispered behind me.

'Yes,' I said.

'I'm cold, Hugh,' she went on.

'We'll go down,' I said, rising heavily to my feet. 'Oh, I'm stiff and sore! Did you hurt yourself, Terry?'

She shook her head.

When we came to the cave I ran in to snatch up my rifle and load it.

'I'll never go out without this again,' I said.

'Why are you loading the rifle? Why are you looking like that?' Terry demanded.

'I'm loading it in case I need it,' I told her grimly. 'What am I looking like?'

'You can't! You can't!' she cried wildly. 'I won't let you do it! I'd rather see us both dead, Hugh—'

'Hush!' I tried to quieten her. 'You're overwrought, Terry. Sit down, lassie, and I'll see about a meal. Take off these wet clothes. Let me look at the scratches you got—'

'I know what you're meaning to do!' she went on without heeding my words. She stared at me for a moment with panic in her eyes.

'You're going to kill! you're going to make murderers of us both.'

'I'm going to defend myself if I must,' I answered.

'No! No! No! No!' she exclaimed. 'You can't do it! I won't let you! Give me the rifle!'

She flung herself on me and began to wrest the rifle from me.

'Let go!' I shouted, 'it's loaded; do you hear, Terry! let it go, it's loaded!'

I had to use my strength brutally before I could loosen her grip on the rifle. Suddenly she let the gun go. My hands were round her wrists and the gun fell clattering to the floor. She began to drag herself back, struggling in intent silence to be free. I gripped her wrists with all my force. Then she let herself fall on the floor beside the rifle, clawing with her fingers towards it. I dragged her to her feet and held her close to me.

She commenced to tremble and shake and her struggling ended.

'Terry!' I breathed. 'What are you doing, Terry?'

'Let me go,' she said in a hoarse voice. 'Take your hands off me.'

'Then let the rifle be,' I retorted. All at once she grew limp. I supported her as best I could with one arm while I let down the hammock with my free hand. I lifted her into the hammock and commenced to take off her wet clothes. I left her there while I blew up the fire. I felt deathly cold; the cave was dank and shadowy; I was afraid I was going to be sick. The rifle lay unheeded on the floor until I tripped over it as I went to bring out the bottle of whisky Duncan gave us. I unloaded the rifle before I poured out some of the whisky into a cup.

'Drink this,' I bade Terry. 'Draw up the blankets and keep yourself warm until your clothes dry.'

She took the cup obediently and swallowed the dram at a gulp. She coughed and tears stood in her eyes.

'It's very strong,' she whispered.

I drank a mouthful of the stuff myself.

'Hugh!' Terry whispered.

'Yes?' I said. 'I'm going to make a meal, Terry. I'm sure you're famished.'

'Come here a minute, Hugh,' she continued. As I came to the side of the hammock she reached out her arms gently and touched my cheeks and my hair with her hands.

'Hugh!' she murmured.

'I'll never forgive myself,' I said.

'I was frightened,' she said. 'There's not much food in the house,' she went on.

'It'll do one meal, surely,' I said. 'I'll soon get more.'

'You can't! you can't!' she cried, 'it's not safe.'

'As safe as starving to death with hunger, Terry.'

She looked carefully all round the cave as if it was strange to her eyes. There was fear in her voice when she looked at me again and asked:

'What men were these, Hugh? Where were they going? What did they look like? Oh, I'm so frightened, Hugh!' she cried in a shaken voice before I could answer her questions. Her voice was loud in the cave.

'But don't be frightened,' I told her. 'What harm can happen to us here? An army couldn't dislodge us from this place. When I get food—'

'You're not going out to-day!' she exclaimed. 'Promise me, Hugh—I won't let you go—don't, don't go!'

'But we need meat,' I reasoned.

'We'll get meat to-morrow,' she said. 'Wait and I'll get up and show you how much we have, plenty to keep us—'

'You'll lie still until the cave warms and your clothes dry,' I answered.

'Then you'll stay at home to-day? Just to-day, promise me, Hugh.'

'Very well then,' I agreed. 'I can wait until to-morrow.'

Yesterday's to-morrow is now to-day, and I have not yet gone to the hill for meat. The cave is as dark and cold as any fireless unillumined hole in the water-dripping rocks could ever be. We have been sitting all day since morning in the dark recess of our cavern, not even daring to go out for water, without fire, or light; the last of our meat is on the table, scraps of grouse and a few ounces of salt venison.

In the morning early when we wakened I started to tell Terry about a very strange dream that my waking interrupted. 'It was as clear as day in my mind when I wakened,' I told her; 'I said to myself; "I'll remember this to tell Terry,"—and now, it's all jumbled up and broken already, and I scarcely remember it at all.'

'Dreams are often like that,' she said. 'Dreams before waking are clear in your head until you try to remember them and speak about them, and then, they're like your face in the water of a pool, when you go close to look at yourself your breath breaks the image and the water ruffles, and it's gone. It'll perhaps come back to you, Hugh, if you don't try to think of it. Oh, how I slept! Like a stone. I didn't dream—'

'I wish I could remember!' I interrupted her; 'it'll bother me all day if I don't recollect what it was about—I think I dreamt it was a dipping-day. I heard sheep and dogs. I don't often hear sounds in a dream—'

'What put a dipping-day into your head, of all strange things?' she asked with a smile.

'Mebbe the dogs yesterday,' I replied.

The smile left her face.

'One thing's clear still,' I continued, 'the bleating of sheep. I can hear it as if it was real—hark! what was that?'

'The wind,' she said, 'It's gone to the east, surely.'

'It wasn't the wind,' I answered; 'no, it wasn't the noise of the wind—oh if that dream would come or go!'

I strained my ears to listen, but the sound that vexed me did not come again.

'I suppose I'd better get up and light the fire and see about some venison,' I went on, and sighed. 'Bed's the best place to-day, Terry! Oh, the east wind! It slackens the marrow of your bones.'

'I'll get up, it's my morning,' she offered, but at her words I jumped out of the hammock and hurried to stir up the fire.

I had scarcely bent over the fireplace when the alien noise that tantalized my ears broke out again.

'Did you hear that?' I asked, straightening myself up and facing her.

'I thought I heard something,' she admitted. 'What was it, Hugh, did you hear it—'

'I heard it,' I answered slowly.

'What was it?'

'Sheep,' I said.

At my words the noise of bleating, borne from the east, swelled up and sounded in our diligent ears.

'Sheep,' I said again. 'My ears are better sleeping than awake, Terry.'

I went to the door of the cave to peer out. I heard Terry scramble from the hammock and in a moment I felt her behind me.

'Keep back,' I warned her.

'Let me see, Hugh,' she said. 'I want to see the sheep.'

I retreated into the cave, taking her with me, and sat down on the edge of the table.

'What did you see?' she insisted. 'Hugh, you must tell me, you can't keep me in ignorance—I'll go myself and look.'

'Stay where you are!' I cried.

'Then tell me. I'm not a fool or a child.'

I took her arm and led her to the door of the cave. We peered out together, over the gorge, down by the loch, and saw on the verge of the moor a drab white moving mass. The bleating of many sheep dinned in our ears.

'No one can see us from there,' Terry whispered.

I shook my head. But venturing to look more incautiously out I caught sight of men in the gully right beneath us, and I dragged Terry back into the cave once more.

'There are men beneath us, not a couple of hundred yards away,' I whispered.

I took the rifle for which we had struggled and filled the magazine examining each shell as I handled it. She stood by without attempting to hinder me.

'What sort of men?' she breathed.

'I'm going to see,' I answered. 'Stay here and don't move. Reach me over that telescope—have you a dry rag?'

I opened the glass and wiped the lenses.

'Don't! don't go out!' Terry implored. 'If they're so near—they'll see you.'

I shook my head.

'They'll never catch sight of me,' I assured her. 'I must see, we must know, we can't stay closed up here like blind moles starting at every sound in ignorance.'

I heard her whisper 'Oh, be careful, Hugh!' as I got down on the floor to crawl from the cave. First behind boulders, then with a heathery ridge to screen me, I squirmed and crept until I reached a coign of vantage from which I could see all ways without being seen. When I looked at the men in the gorge I saw them through a narrow slit between two stones, and their gaze, even if it directed itself straight at the place where I lay, could not possibly distinguish me between the contiguous rocks that made a loophole for my rifle and my eyes. The bulging cliff hid me from above, and the east was empty until the sheep, still far away, warned me of danger; so from the east I could not be seen unless I let an enemy come close; I gripped the rifle when that thought struck me; we dared not let men discover our place. But the east was vacant except for the distant sheep, and I turned to look straight down at the men in the ravine. I laid the telescope open beside me. I could distinguish the strangers only too plainly without its aid. There were two of them and they advanced until they were a short distance west of the cave, and there they halted. One of them began to sweep the country with binoculars. In spite of the security of my hiding-place I huddled down when he turned his attention to the hill-side where I crouched, and the cliff above me. A hundred things that might betray us presented themselves to my mind. I saw our manifold traces everywhere about us; it seemed impossible that he could avoid seeing what was so patent to my own imagination. With the open sky over me and the rock looming above I felt as if I was lying in plain

view. I could not forbear casting my eyes to the east whence
the noise of bleating sheep came with increased force.

That fit of panic ceased. I gathered courage to look forth
again at the intruders. The fellow with the binoculars had
apparently satisfied himself, for he now sat on a boulder
with his back to me watching his companion hunt around
for dead heather and bits of stick carried by the autumn
gales from our birch wood. My heart came into my mouth
when I saw this fellow fling down a handful of sticks beside
the boulder on which his comrade sat and point to the cluster
of trees west of our cave. If he went there for wood we were
lost. Our peat-stack, our paths, must betray us. But the
man on the boulder commenced to speak vehemently. I
could hear the angry tones of his voice, he was so loud
and near, though I failed to distinguish his words. He
gesticulated with his arms, pointing in all directions, but
chiefly to the north-east; the noise of sheep swelled into a
great lamentation. Eventually he jumped hastily to his feet
and ran to the side of the burn in the gorge where he pointed
at the ground and kicked something embedded in the moss.
The other fellow bent submissively to wrench a fir root from
the boggy ground. I was glad we had gone farther for our
roots. They lit a fire and he with the binoculars returned to
his seat on the stone.

They had a tattered and desperate air that daunted me.
The one who seemed to be leader, and sat like a graven
statue on the boulder, staring across the gorge and down the
lochside to the moor, had a rifle slung over his shoulder;
his binoculars-case was slung round his neck and dangled on
his chest where it came easily to his hand. He was wearing a
khaki jacket and grey trousers. I strained my eyes searching
for the gleam of brass buttons on his jacket. I could not
distinguish whether there were none, or if they had been
blackened, but that single detail did more to impress me
and fill me with forebodings than all the other signs of
hazard that the men's manner and clothes betrayed.

The companion of this armed man, more ragged and fierce
in appearance than his leader, seemed far less dangerous. He

was a large slouching creature, black-bearded and red-faced.
His cap was drawn down over one eye, his jacket, too large
even for his frame, was turned up at the wrists and I could
see the lining above his hands. He had a furtive gait. He
was for ever turning his large head over his shoulder and
as he fed the fire he started every few moments to snatch
up his rifle from where it lay on the ground, like one in
constant fear.

When the fire was burning well he produced a bundle
wrapped in a red cloth, a handkerchief perhaps, from his
pocket. He unfolded the bundle and when he had made a
sharp point on a birch branch he speared the contents of
his bundle on this stake and held whatever he was cooking
in the flame of the fire. Very soon the savour of burning
meat came to my nostrils and in a little while they were
eating ravenously. My own hunger rose as I watched them
and smelled their food. I could hear Terry whispering:

'Hugh! Hugh!'

I retreated to the cave. We stayed the worst pangs of our
hunger with scraps of grouse while I told her what I saw.

'We must get food or starve,' I said.

'Can't we light a fire?' she asked. She was shuddering
with cold.

'You should go to bed and keep yourself warm there,' I
advised her.

'I can't go to bed,' she broke out. 'Oh! I wish I could
get warm!'

While the two men were eating the noise of sheep continued without seeming to come any nearer. I looked through
the glass from the mouth of our cave. I could see the sheep
plainly at the far end of Loch Coulter; they were huddled
in a mass while dogs, whose yelping we heard occasionally,
ran in circles round the flock. I saw a group of men seated
to the left of the sheep, and I fancied I saw a thin spire
of smoke rising from amongst them. One man stood alone
by himself, away from his companions to the right of the
sheep, outlined on a hillock as if he were standing sentinel
there.

'Can you see anything?' Terry whispered. 'Give me the glass.'

I gave her the glass without a word. She stared through it for a long time.

'What does it mean?' she asked at length. 'What men are these?'

'It means we might have been less scrupulous about taking a sheep,' I answered. 'It means mischief.'

Half an hour later the crowd of men began to rise from sitting amongst the heather; they dispersed: some went behind the sheep, others came in front, the flock moved slowly west. I ventured to look down into the gully. The two men there had risen. They were standing together and he with the binoculars gazed backwards at the sheep. He spoke to his companion who scattered the fire and stamped its embers into the ground. Then they walked up the valley and shortly disappeared.

The sheep approached. Their bleating resounded amongst the cliffs. With yelping dogs hurrying them, and half a dozen armed desperadoes leading them and following them, they passed beneath us, following these two, their apparent vanguard, into the west. The cave was bitterly cold. We were famished with hunger and racked with fears. We could scarcely restrain ourselves from lighting a fire until the sheep were out of sight. Then I took the water-pail.

'Risk or not, we can't let ourselves perish of hunger and cold,' I declared. 'Light the fire, Terry. They're gone, all out of sight.'

I had barely left the cave when I was inside again shouting, 'Put out that fire, put it out!'

We dragged the flaming sticks upon the floor and beat them out.

Terry was white and shaking. When the fire was extinguished I began to tremble myself.

'There's a rearguard too,' I said hoarsely.

'Did they—did they see you?' she asked.

'I don't know—they were almost on me—one on each side of the valley—walking along the hill-sides—'

I sat in the mouth of the cave with my rifle across my knee.
A long time passed before I ventured to look out. Night was
drawing near, dull, cold, and ominous. I could see no signs
of men. We lighted our fire and Terry used some of our
dear stores making a meal. I grudged each mouthful that
I ate, yet my ravening hunger mocked my scruples and my
fears for the future. We were wrapt in misery like a cloak,
hungry and cold and weak with spent fears. There may be
a pike on my set-line. I shall go down when night comes,
dark, safe, dear night.

'I must get meat to-morrow, come what will,' I said.

'We must have meat soon,' Terry agreed. And then,
spreading out her hands to the fire she laughed, and said,
'Oh, fire, I love you.'

I HAVE BEEN listening to the quiet all day. Everything is as it was before these men appeared, the country empty, winter on the hills and autumn ageing in the valleys. Terry is here, here beside me where I can touch her and, turning to look at her, smile when she smiles. We have lighted our fire and laid on peats. The cave is warm. The rabbit I killed this morning beside Loch Coulter makes a fine smell as it braises in a pot.

This is our country. I feel, not as if strangers had intruded on our peace, but as if we had erred into another dangerous land, and now we have come home. Yesterday is a tale of a thousand years ago. For all my looking back, and recalling, it will not be brought near, but like a scene viewed through the wrong end of a telescope, its events are distant and impersonal, clear and crowded and far away. I cannot see myself in them as this thing myself that sits listening to the sounds of our frosty autumn day. I see pigmy figures toiling over hills, running, falling, one dying; they are not human; not I but a marionette effigy of myself am amongst them. I begin to speak about that man, and as I speak I try to feel horror. I should feel horror, and I feel none.

Terry says, 'It was you or him, your life or his.'

Truly, I feel no horror. When I have twinges in my wounded side I do not recollect immediately how I was hurt, or when. I shall go up to-night and hide him in a sepulchre of stones from the eagle and the hoodie and the scavenging hinds.

I can feel Terry's eyes on me. I think she believes I am horror-struck and hiding it from her. If I tell her that my

135

mind is free she thinks I am saying it to convince and comfort her.

It is bitter to feel her pitiful eyes on me and to watch the distress she tries in vain to hide, knowing as I do that I do not require pity, and that she is unhappy because she imagines I am in despair. How can I despair, or simulate that hideous horror that I ought to feel, I a murderer, and at peace? I long to persuade her that I am not hiding my horror from her.

We are seldom of separate minds. We think alike, we think together. Now we are divided and I lack companionship. Maybe she feels I ought to speak to her, sharing my woe. How can I speak things I do not feel, or unburden my mind of a trouble that does not beset me? Perhaps she like myself is miserable because we are divided. If I could say the things she imagines I long to say—I try saying them to myself. They sound false and forced to my own ear. It's beyond me to ape horror and anguish of mind. I feel nothing but my tired limbs and the stabbing of my wounded side, and this quiet rediscovered country where we live.

And if by speaking I could persuade her that I feel no blood-guiltiness, how would she regard me then? I recall the day when she caught the rifle and tried to take it from me. If I said that the picture of that man falling was before my mind's eye like the fall of a tree, as casual, as unconcerned with mortality, with what grievous eyes would she see me? I dare not, I dare not speak. I'm not a monster, surely, callous to human death; to kill a man and feel no anguish—I have felt worse pangs when a stag died in a froth of its own blood than I feel now. His blood's on my sleeve, with my own.

Or is this my present state of mind nothing but a hiatus between deed and thought. If I could speak to her, and hear her speak again, I'd know. She waits for my words, I am silent, night is approaching when I must take stones and hide the dead body of the man I killed. I see him fall, before my eyes, like a tree falling, slowly at first, then in sudden collapse. His outstretched arm flings the rifle away;

the fingers of his outstretched arm extend themselves; to close and grasp the moss where he falls. I never knew dead men's eyes stared like his; it was foolish of me to imagine that dead men's eyes closed when death struck them blind; death has fingers for the heart alone; how many stags I've seen with glazing eyes, and tapped their eyeballs with the blade of a knife, before I bled them. I should have known. I'll close his eyes, when I hap him in stones to keep him from the hoodie and the eagle. Upon the flat hill-top, under the sky, with my fingers on the eyelids of the man I killed, I'll surely know then what I am.

Then I can speak, and Terry will answer me. I pray for horror to compass me. Come, night, dark minister of time.

It is only two days since I waited at the door of the cave and the sheep and men went past. When all had gone and were lost in the west I spied every corner of the country, sweeping it yard by yard with the telescope. Night came soon. We slept ill; the rifle lay beside me all night. In the morning I took it in my hands.

'I'm going for a beast, sheep or deer or goat, I care not which,' I told Terry.

'Is it safe?' she asked anxiously.

'Safe?' I laughed. 'Fully as safe as dying of hunger here, like rats in a trap, Terry.'

'Let me tidy up the cave first,' she said. 'Then it'll be ready for us when we come back.'

'But you're not coming,' I told her.

She nodded her head vehemently.

'Terry,' I went on, 'you must attend to me—'

'And let you go out of my sight, maybe never to come again!' She cried frantically. 'I know there's danger, Hugh. I can see it in your eyes, your face. I feel it in my heart. Look at me! look at me and say there's no danger—you can't hide it! I'm going with you! Oh, Hugh, if anything happened to you—'

'What could happen?' I interrupted. 'Listen to me, Terry, you *must* be reasonable. We need food, we've got to get it, whatever comes. One can stalk a stag more easily than two. If there's danger, two people on the hill make the risk double what it is for one. One can watch better than two, one can escape faster than two, one can hide more securely than two—'

She was silent for a space, staring at me.

'Show me how to work the rifle,' she said at last in a low voice. 'Is Duncan's rifle loaded? Leave it with me.'

She put her arms round my neck and kissed me.

'You had better go quickly,' she said.

'I'll be home soon. Stay inside the cave and don't wander from it, whatever happens,' I said.

'Come quickly, come home quickly, Hugh,' she bade me. 'I'll be waiting for you. I'll watch for you with Duncan's glass.'

I took my own .303, and a score of bullets. Then I spied for deer from beside the cave and found a herd about two miles away on the hill across the gorge. I showed them to Terry.

'Good luck,' she said.

The wind was right and if only I could cross the valley without being seen the rest of the stalk was child's play. I needed to do no more than slant up the hill towards a ridge west of the herd. The wind remained easternly. It had brought many beasts to this corner of the hills. I saw half a dozen herds scattered here and there, but those I saw first were nearest and most convenient.

The beasts of this herd were restless and I saw them raise their heads from eating to gaze downhill; I attributed their restlessness to the season of the year and the disturbance of the previous day. I crept and slid down the hill with my eyes on my quarry, ready to freeze at the first sign of their perceiving me. The morning sun, weak though it was, shone in their eyes and kept me hid. I reached the bottom of the slough without attracting their attention. I glanced upwards at the cave. I could not see Terry though I knew she had her eyes on me, and when I realized how easy it was for a man to lie in hiding, watching me, himself unseen, I spied the country once more. Then I thought that no stranger would come into this place expecting to find people in it. Only the wildest chance could show me to an intruder before I saw him. At that the tussocks and black patches of bog which had seemed so like men reassumed their old innocent character. All was quiet. The deer in front of me were eating. Occasionally a stag roared. We could not kill many more stags, except young beasts, for their roaring was that of beasts nearly spent. I crept under the brow of the hill and commenced to go up in a long circuit towards the ridge I had chosen for a lair when I came near enough to shoot. I climbed slowly, conserving my energy. I was not tired but empty. I could not think of food without repugnance. Nevertheless I was weak from lack of food. When I tried to hurry I grew dizzy. It cost me an hour to reach the level of the deer, a distance I had often covered in twenty minutes. I sheltered behind a rock to make certain that my rifle was loaded, and that its barrel had not become choked with moss and peat-dust while I was crawling.

I stood up cautiously to look round the edge of the rock at the herd. All at once I heard a noise behind me. I was shaking like a leaf with the excitement which always seizes me when I am hunting and come near beasts without yet reaching a place from which to shoot. But as I swung round to meet the noise I ceased to tremble; my nerves were strung like a taut bow; my right hand turned the safety catch and the rifle came to my side at the ready; its muzzle swung until it pointed directly at a man less than a hundred yards away. We stared at each other for what seemed an eternal space. I was conscious of nothing in the world but this man, facing me, with his rifle, like my own, pointed at me, and my breathful lungs. I saw him with more clarity than anything else has ever shown. I saw his white face and his tattered clothes and the bandolier slung across his chest. I saw his bare head and the wind blowing its unkempt black hair. The rifle swung up to his shoulder and its sound crashed out in my face. I felt something tug at my side; blinding rage swept over me. I flung myself on my face in the lee of the rock and as I reached the ground I fired. He was drawing back the bolt

of his rifle to reload when I fired. How could I miss? he
was foursquare before me, a broader target than any stag or
hind. I had reloaded and my rifle was trained on his chest
before he moved again. I waited for him to send the bolt
home. I would not fire till he was ready. His right hand
went to his throat, his left arm, gripping the rifle by the
stock, extended slowly. His head fell back and his mouth
opened. As his left arm stretched out to its full length the
rifle flung from his grasp; he took a short step forward and
stumbled, the fingers of his left hand spread out like a fan;
he began to fall, slowly; and then he pitched on his face.
The smell of cordite was in my nostrils; I was half drunk
with the noise of my rifle and the smell of powder; fierce
exultation filled me. I heard the clip of deer's hooves over
stones; my breath went out with a gusty sound. I thought,
it happened in the time of drawing a breath. I got up and
leaned against the rock. I was shaking now; my limbs felt
cold. There was a burning in my lungs and a nausea in my
stomach as if I had run up a steep brae until breath and
strength failed. I took my telescope from its case to train
it on my enemy. He lay as he fell. I walked towards him,
stumbling as I went. My nerveless fingers would scarcely
hold the rifle.

I stood over him, staring down at his broad back. His
face had fallen into a mossy pool, the fingers of his left
hand clutched the moss and short-cropped grass; he had
a heavy gold ring on the forefinger of his left hand. It shone
amongst the yellowing grass. Blood stained the hand at his
throat and darkened his jacket sleeve. I heard a shout far
away beneath me, and looking in the direction of the noise
I saw several tiny figures climbing up the hill towards me.
A bullet splattered on a stone and screamed over my head.
The shrill whine of the ricochet was still in my ears when
the voice of a rifle followed its messenger. I ran to snatch
the dead man's rifle from where it lay. I aimed it downhill
and emptied its magazine at my pursuers as fast as I could
work the bolt. I laughed to see them halt and scatter, and
take refuge behind stones. A fusillade of slots answered me

without giving me any feeling of danger. I trailed the body of my enemy over on his back and tore the bandolier from his chest. His cheeks were wet and dirty with the water of the pool, his eyes outstared the sky. I could not make myself lay fingers on his eyelids to close his eyes. He had a satchel by his side. I flung it and the bandolier of cartridges across my own shoulder. I took the bolt from his rifle and dropped it into a marshy hag where it would sink, never to be found, and flung his rifle into another pool. It was a .303, like my own. My hands were imbrued with blood.

Bullets screamed overhead. I cast a final glance at my pursuers from the lee of a boulder. They had given up shouting to conserve their breath for the ascent. I had no fear of them. I knew the country too well to be overtaken or driven into a corner. I had only a vague plan in my head, to lead them on until it was dark, to draw them far away from this part of the country and then, eluding them, to return.

My fingers, groping in the dead man's satchel, brought forth a thick bannock of oatcake and a lump of cheese. I commenced to trot in a southernly direction, intending to follow the south shoulder of Meall na Ceardaich until it rose again to Carn na Ceardaich. If I had not lost my pursuers by then, I could double across the Farrow and lead them through the wilderness of the Durc until nightfall. I ate from the satchel as I went. But I had not gone a mile when I felt unaccountably weak; my breath laboured; I put my left hand on my hip to steady my breathing. My fingers felt sticky. When I brought them before my eyes they were red with blood. I stood like a fool, gazing at my hand. Panic took hold of me. I cast around for a boulder behind which I could hide and defend myself to the last. In a moment I recovered myself by force of will from that mood of despair. I thought of Terry waiting for my return. I unfastened my jacket and pulled up my shirt until I saw my side. It was dark with half-dried blood and a narrow red line of new blood marked where the bullet struck me. I put my fingers in the wound. It was long but not deep, a raking slash in the flesh. When I had soaked my handkerchief in a little burn I washed the wound roughly and made a pad with the handkerchief to lay along my side. I pressed my cap over the pad, under my shirt, and brought my belt up and drew it as tight round the wound as I could bear. The belt was broad enough to keep the bandage in place if it did not slip. I dragged my trousers in until the top button-hole of the spare reached the first braces' button. I was not wearing braces. I could run now. I glanced over my shoulder. Six men, spread out in a semicircle, were behind me, less than a mile away. I knew that they were winded after their climb. I believed I could escape. I made more easternly, in the direction of Loch Ericht where there were woods to hide me if I reached them. As I fled I spoke to myself, urging myself on, advising myself of the way, and the obstacles in front of me. I heard myself crying, 'Don't be afraid, Terry.' And then I said, 'Hugh! Hugh! hurry! you must take them away from the cave, you must lead them away from the cave.' It made a refrain to my running. I did not feel pain or fear or weakness while that aim was in my mind. An occasional shot warned me that I had not shaken off pursuit. At such times my thoughts took a start. I knew I was not fit to race up steep ground. I knew I dared not let myself be herded into a narrow valley where my foes, speeding downhill, would come near enough to pick me off as I laboured up the other side. I swung to the left, following the ridges of Carn na Ceardaich without ever glancing behind. Suddenly a loud 'Halloo!' almost beneath me brought me to a standstill. I caught sight of a man in the valley of the Sluie burn. The fleetest of my pursuers, on the right wing of their chase, had outdistanced me. If his plan was to cut me off from Loch Ericht's refuge-woods and force me into haggy flats where I would find no shelter, it seemed to have succeeded. I was tempted to lie down and wait until I was overtaken. I could defend myself even against half a dozen men. Rage began to swell in me against the men who chased me like a beast before them. Yet I remembered Terry once more. As I looked down at the swift fellow who had outrun me hope revived. He was pelting down the valley at top speed as if he imagined I was right before him. I could neither see nor hear anything of his companions. It seemed to me that he had outdistanced them and broken their cordon by his haste. It was my only chance. I was standing on the lip of a little corrie which fell to the Sluie. Once I reached that burn there was nothing but level moor between me and Loch Ericht. I bolted into the shallow shelter of the corrie. Half a mile down it began to grow narrow; the stream which drained it had gouged out a ravine. I was barely into the bed of the stream when shouts broke forth above me on the hill-top. I crouched as low as I could while a figure on the skyline shouted as if to the man below and waved his arm eastward. Immediately he vanished I toiled down the gorge. Sometimes I slipped and fell feet foremost over slippery rocks; I plunged down gravel slides which fell with me, filling my boots with sand and stones. A rock struck my side and I lay gasping with agony. Warm blood trickled down my side. Still I kept on. In a short time my enemies must find that I was not before them. They had followed me too far to let me hope that they would abandon the chase because I had given them the slip. The ravine spread into a dell. I scampered across it to reach the Sluie and climb the opposite bank. Startled cries told me that I was seen. I fled without attempting to hide, towards Loch Ericht. I was barely a quarter of a mile in front of my foremost pursuers when I crossed the deer-fence into the wood. I took my rifle in my hand as I clambered over the fence. I steadied myself to aim at the leading man. I may have hit him. He flung himself down with a savage cry, and I, with a yell of exultation and mockery more savage than his, burst into the wood whose thickets no enemy would dare to thread for fear of ambush.

Climbing steadily upwards on a long slant which would bring me into the cavernous rocks of the Farrow, I harkened for the noise of pursuit. No sound followed me. I was safe at last. Yet now that I had reached my goal I was afraid. The wood was filled with lurking dangers, each tree made a convenient ambuscade. I dared not halt to attend to my wound but pressed on as if the route was yelling at my heels. I was running like a fool by the time I came to the head of the wood.

I crept into a rocky cavern from whose shelter I could survey the land. It was deserted and so quiet I could scarcely believe that those wild voices which followed me had ever existence outside a dream. It was bitterly cold. When I had eaten some more oatcakes and made a pad for my wound with my shirt I lay down on the earth to wait for night. Cold and pain and hunger come at length to be their own anodyne. I thought drowsily of our cave, warmly lit, of Terry waiting until I came.

At night's approach I left my hiding-hole. I was dead-tired and every limb ached so that it was torture to move and drag my leaden feet over the Farrow, through fresh snow. I made a circuit by the Durc and the head of the Sluie burn in case my enemies were still loitering by the lower course of the stream. Night had fallen before I neared the cave. My tiredness left me as I came to our gorge. I ran up the steep slope saying, 'Terry! Terry! Terry!' over and over again under my breath, not loud, for fear I warned a lurking foe and startled her. I felt for the entrance to the cave with my hand. I rested a moment, leaning against the rock, while I drew a great breath of gladness to be home. I whispered, 'Terry! Terry! are you there? It's Hugh!'

No answer came. I noticed how dark and still the cave was. I thought, 'She's gone to bed. She's sleeping.' I was angry because she had fallen asleep, forgetting me. I said, 'I wouldn't have fallen asleep waiting for you, Terry.' I cried, 'Terry! are you sleeping?' No voice replied. I groped my way into the cave until I reached the hammock. It was slung close to the wall. I cried, 'Terry!' and then in a louder voice I shouted her name, bidding her speak to me. My loud breath beat on the walls of rock whose echoing voice flung back her name and the night resounded with a mockery of my fear. I stumbled to the fireplace to plunge my hand in the ashes of the fire. I waited for the exquisite pain of burning to abate my dread. The ashes were cold.

I could not think clearly. My head reeled and if I had not

clutched the mantelshelf I would have fallen. I shivered like
a man in a fever and when I tried to speak, to cry, to shout
her name that the whole world must hear and echo my calling
voice, I had no voice; my mouth opened and closed, making
no sound, only my breath broke and sighed in my throat and
my heart, as loud in my ears as thunder, seemed to grow and
swell in my bosom. I drove myself outside. When I shouted,
the hills bandied her name. Poised on the brink of despair I
listened with bated breath for her replying voice. I began to
speak aloud to her, scolding her, petting her, begging her
to come home. Now I fell into a rage against the men who
followed me. I rushed back to the cave for the rifle and
brandished it, cursing them, threatening them, until dread
mastered me once more. Then I cried, 'Terry! Terry!
come home.'

Through all the moments of that time something in my
head, cold and malignant and as serene as the dead, heard
my foolish voice's babbling as if it was a child's wailing, and
knew that this my noise was but the momentary extravagance
of fear. And as it knew, so I was aware with part of my mind
that when I gave up shouting for Terry who would not come,
never come home, this frozen rage would rule me, this icy
death in life be my portion. I clung to my fear, lest it leave
me to despair. I shouted when I knew calling was vain. But
still I shouted to keep myself from despair.

The night was still, no voice answering broke its quiet.
My heart was dead in me. I went listlessly into the cave
for firewood. I began to make a bonfire at the mouth of
the cave. I became engrossed in what I was doing, still
evading thought. The wood blazed up into a beacon that
miles around must see. I piled on more fuel. I exulted to
think my enemies would see the blaze. When they came
to me, I would be prepared to meet them. I laid the rifle
I carried beside the fire while I went into the cave, now
brightly illumined, to bring out the other guns. I found
only the .22. Duncan's rifle had disappeared. I searched
frantically for it, flinging the bedclothes on the floor, tearing
things from their place, to discover it. I could not come on

it. As I searched I fancied I heard the sound of a voice above the din of the fire. I rushed outside to listen. I retreated away from the fire, into the darkness, out of range of its sound, to attend for that voice. I heard it a second time, like my own name feebly called. With a glad heart I answered, 'Terry!' I plunged down the hill to find her. I was not tired any more. I took her in my arms and carried her up the slope. The fire made so loud a wind of flame that I scarcely heard my own voice murmuring, 'Terry, Terry, Terry.'

She lay with closed eyes in my arms. Her wan pinched face was streaked with the dirt of bogs, her clothes were sopping wet. I felt no weariness nor pain in my limbs. I could have waited for ever by the fire, gazing at her face, with my arms supporting her. She opened her eyes to look up at me. I took her wet clothes from her and rubbed her chilled limbs with my hands, chafing them until they were warm as mine.

'You were away a long, long time,' she whispered once. She was asleep in my arms before ever I got her into the hammock. Once or twice in the night she wakened with a cry of fear and clung to me more tightly. I did not dare move or rise to put out the fire for fear of waking her. I could not sleep, I was too glad to sleep.

I killed a rabbit early this morning. We have a day's food at least, and a day's respite before I need go out to kill a stag for meat.

'We've only each other,' Terry said when she wakened. 'If anything happens, I hope it'll be soon, and both of us together.'

'Nothing's going to happen,' I tried to assure her. 'Nothing.'

Nothing. Nothing came to him and he's nothing, the man I killed. I washed his blood from my hands, his blood and my own. Blood will have blood they say.

She dressed my side. The bullet carried some cloth into the wound. I think it is clean now. I've been watching a hoodie on the other hill, near where he lies. Maybe I'm too late to close his eyes.

I THINK WE were never so happy as now. We have made up our minds and chosen a course; we have escaped from doubt. The fears that afflicted us since we came to this place are gone from mind like the cold and hunger and fatigue of the past few days. We are not anxious or afraid any more. We have found surer peace in the time of the racked world's anguish than ever pleased us while the earth was quiet.

I can scarcely take my eyes from Terry as she bends over the poor dying creature in our hammock. She has been standing there, still as a statue, for a long time. Her face is radiant, her eyes shine. Happiness burns in me as I watch her. Often I rise from where I sit writing to go beside her. He is almost gone, the gaunt lines of his famished cheeks are growing smoother. His vast eyes stay on Terry's face. They are free from terror at last. When I look at him, and see his thin hands lying on the bedclothes, I turn my back in momentary shame that ever I feared this frail thing whose passing breath, no louder than a sigh, marks an end to our life here. Shame does not endure; we have helped him, and ourselves, and the days of our fear are spent.

Though the cave is warm and bright I can think of leaving its comfort without a pang. It served its purpose, it sheltered us and brought us to know ourselves and chose the only way of peace. When I remember the months that we have spent here I do not grudge their alarms and dangers, but rather I am grateful for that harsh instruction because it taught us wisdom and gave us happiness beyond fear and thought of our own safety.

I gaze at Terry's pitiful face. If I had not her, what a poor
tormented thing I'd be, like the forlorn man who dies in our
bed. I have no courage, save with her, no wisdom that is not
hers, no hope, no life except in her. Oh, Terry! Terry!
I'd live a million years and suffer all that time can inflict to
reach a moment such as this.

The shortening day is done. When he's past the reach of
hunger we'll go carrying what we can, to meet our fellows.
To suffer is happiness, if we go rightly.

The past had no shape or form until now. But like slaves
who toil without aim or end in view, we were rapt in
trivial moments. I review the completed past; it glows
in my memory. The jewelled summer shows itself again;
I remember how we bathed and played at gathering berries
in the bright hot weeks when every creature was young.
Summer's a lovely dream; hardships and fret remove
themselves from knowledge. I'll sleep to-night and forget
summer. When I waken, it'll be there, and Terry dancing
by the loch.

Though we depart, leaving our cave to the fox or the wild
cat or the cleanly badger, this place, this land, is ours, and
we, tied to it as the wild creatures are, cannot escape from it
by going. But we belong to it, we have given ourselves up to
it; no other abode can ever break this strange allegiance. We
make ourselves its servants by going. The fire blazes finely,
we've no need to spare our sticks or hide our presence. The
hill-world that encloses our hearts was good to us. We owe
a duty to that which gave us fire and food and brings forth
creatures like ourselves, human folk to help.

We have escaped from fear, from anger too, and grief,
and horror. Nothing is left but pity. The man who lies
dying in our bed makes a symbol of humanity for us.
How can we fear or hate broken men like him, whose
works, that grieved us when we saw our garden wasted,
are done in anguish and despair. Dangerous like trapped
beasts, destroying because they fear destruction, hunting
fugitives to death because death halloos at their own heels,
murdering and stealing in dread of murder at men's hands

or from the ravening rage of hunger, they are not things to
fear and hate, but men to pity.

The past resolves itself out of broken events into a pattern.
All the stages of our progress to this moment lose their
separate selves in it; they take meaning and relevance from
it, assuming the aspect of necessity. Necessity does not admit
grief to rule. What we suffered seems now an apprenticeship
merely. I remember our wasted garden, without grief, and
the days of our flight, without dismay. I do not hate the men
who hunted me nor suffer horror when I recall the man I
killed. *He* came to the place of his death where I killed him,
I but the instrument of that power which carries men out of
fear and rage to pity.

I piled a cairn of stones over him. I said as I heaped stone
on stone, I'll see this cairn every day on the ridge of the hill.
Nevertheless I went on raising a memorial to affront my eyes.
I could not leave him with a shallow covering of earth and flat
stones, so open to the sky. The crows had picked his eyes
from their sockets. With his eyes gone he did not seem like
a man. I never wondered what man he was, what brought
him here. I piled a great cairn over him. I delved my arms
into the bog where I sunk his rifle to lay it beside him. As
I worked I twisted my side and the wound opened again.

I killed a roe-buck on the morning of the 6th. We were
lucky to get it. I could not have gone far for meat. We
were faint with hunger. I had lost a great deal of blood and
the pain of the wound sapped my strength. I spied the roe
drinking by Loch Coulter and brought him down with the
.22. Terry fried his liver straightaway. Our force renewed
as we ate though we had to compel ourselves to eat.

'It was a lucky chance, getting him,' Terry said, and then,
'He won't last us very long, Hugh.'

'No,' I agreed. 'We must get a stag as soon as possible,
and lay up a store of meat.'

Her eyes kept their distraught look. I found her gazing
at me as if she doubted my presence. I avoided speaking
about the past days.

'Is it—is it safe to go out?' she asked.

I could not tell the lie I wished to tell with her eyes beseeching me. I shook my head.

'Nothing's safe any more,' I said wearily.

'Whatever will happen to us!' she burst out. 'What can we do?'

What could I say that would quieten her fear? I started to skin the roe.

'We'll rest to-morrow,' I declared. 'I'm not fit to go out yet—this filthy wound aches—'

We were like people in a stupor, sleeping, waking to eat, crouching over the fire. The days were growing colder. We could not get warm. Drizzling rain fell, sleet on the tops. In the evening of the 7th I fetched down the rifles. I had even omitted to clean them.

'We'll try for a stag to-morrow,' I said. 'We've had a lesson not to let ourselves run short of food—'

'Dear lesson!' she interrupted bitterly. 'I'm going with you, Hugh.'

I did not argue with her. I could not bear to think of losing her again. Next day, before it was fully light, we carried our store of ammunition and the most precious of our belongings from the cave to hide them in a deep cleft in the rock. We covered them with stones. That was the morning of the 8th of October. Yesterday.

'No one will find them there,' I told Terry.

'Will any one find the cave? Is that what you mean?' she asked breathlessly.

'There's a chance of that,' I returned. 'No more chances—'

'Would you like me to stay—in the cave—guarding it?' she whispered.

'No,' I said.

We went out, she carrying Duncan's rifle and I the .303, in the direction of Meall nan Eacan. We killed a stag before midday. We had a piece of boiled venison with us and we sat down on a ridge overlooking the gorge of our cave to eat it. The damp gusty day showed signs of blowing clear. We sheltered behind a stone with our stag beside us. When we had eaten I commenced to cut up the stag. Its head was off when Terry cried:

'Hugh! listen!'

I started up to hear the unmistakable clamour of rifles echoing amongst the rocks above Loch Coulter. I took the telescope. Before it was focused the noise came again, louder and nearer. I caught sight of dark figures running along the shore of the loch.

'Do you see anything?' Terry demanded. 'What do you see?'

I pushed the glass back into its case.

'See!' I said, pointing out the hurrying specks.

'Men running! Hugh—we can't stay here! they'll be on us!'

'Where'll we go that's safer than the place where we are?' I asked. 'Home to our cave, Terry?'

'We can't stay here,' she went on wildly.

'As well here as anywhere,' I returned. 'How do we know what's happening behind us, by the Sluie, or on the Farrow?'

While we spoke the figures sped on until they were inside the ravine of our cave. Bursts of rifle-fire accompanied them. Soon we could distinguish a dozen men in a scattered company retreating up the gorge while behind them a larger band followed as if in pursuit. I felt my heart begin to race; my hands were shaking with excitement.

'They're fighting!' Terry said in a low voice.

'Yes,' I agreed; 'they're fighting.'

The pursued began to spread out up both sides of the gully. We saw them ensconce themselves behind stones, and their rifles, which they had not paused to use until now, answered the rifles of their pursuers.

'Oh, it's horrible! horrible! men killing each other like beasts!' Terry whispered, covering her face with her hands.

The pursuers halted before the fire of their opponents. One fell, another stumbled like a man struck. They began to run aimlessly, half-retreating. But a voice rang out calling single words of command. In a moment the imminent rout was stayed, and the large company extended itself to face the entrenched enemy, but in a wider arc; the wings raced up the hill-sides.

'They're outflanking them!' I cried when I saw two men of the pursuing troop work their way from stone to stone farther and farther up each side of the ravine without seeming to attract the attention of the fugitives.

'They could get them now!' I cried, wild with excitement, as the wings exposed themselves on a bare burnt patch. 'Oh, the fools! fools! One man on each hill-top will pick them off like sheep!'

I swung round to find Terry regarding me strangely.

'I can't bear to see the weaker side destroy itself,' I muttered.

'They're lost,' she said suddenly. 'They're lost.'

The wings of the large band opened a careful fire at the men beneath them. Two fellows rose convulsively from behind their boulders to fall in a heap.

'It's more than I can endure!' Terry cried. 'Can't we go—out of sight—of this horror!'

'We daren't move,' I returned in a low voice. 'If we lie quiet they'll pass us by—it's our only chance of escape—'

Meanwhile two men who lay side by side in the centre of the pursuit were dragging themselves forward, and as they advanced they carried with them something whose nature I could not distinguish. I began to take the glass from its case to discover what it was they brought so carefully and with such deadly slow intent. They halted and seemed to work busily upon this thing. Then one of them raised his head and the stuttering of a Lewis gun broke out, muted and softened by distance but terrifying still. I slipped the glass into its case again; I had no need to spy now that the noise told me what I had seen them carry. In the uproar of the Lewis gun the crackle of the rifles was drowned, and the interval between each burst seemed a dead silence. Its gunners had found a comfortable stance; they lay steady, sweeping their enemies' line. I could trace the course of their

fire by the flashes that streamed from the gun-muzzle, now
to one hill-slope, now to the other. The defenders broke in
panic. They ran for their lives, flinging their rifles away,
forgetting everything but fear of the machine-gun.

One of the men with the Lewis gun now sprang to his
feet. His clear voice called his band to pursue, his arms
waved them on. His companion, still lying prone, loosed
his weapon on the fugitives. It coughed and barked and
thunderous echoes rolled from hill to hill.

I spared a glance for the broken mob of fugitives who
raced westwards; they surely did not know the country.
Ardverikie fence had to be crossed, and if their foes let them
pass that obstacle they came into boggy country where they
could be cut down at leisure. I caught sight of a lagging
figure in this band who did not fly in blind panic like his
fellows; he glanced backwards, he kept his rifle. When
the leader of the other company leapt on a stone to urge
his followers forward this man dropped behind a hillock.
He crept back to meet his foes until he could just see
them over the ridge of his hillock. His rifle went forward,
steadied, aimed. The leader on the stone was falling before
I heard the shot. The marksman stood up to wave his rifle
defiantly at the enemy. The attackers wavered, with their
eyes on their leader's stricken body. If the other side had
turned now they might have saved the day. But they were
in headlong flight and the remaining Lewis gunner had time
to take his friend's place. He shouted a hoarse command;
hoarser cries answered him. The victorious company raced
after their foes. Now and then a rifle cracked. The fugitives
floundered; they saw the fence too late and attempted to
swerve up the hill; they were killed before they ascended
a couple of hundred yards. I saw one man stumble and
fall. Two of his hunters were on him like hounds. A rifle
swung up, its butt fell with a noise like an axe. The thing
on the ground squirmed convulsively. His assailants flung
themselves on him as if they must finish their work before his
life was fully sped. In a moment they rose, one brandishing
two rifles, the other casting what appeared to be a haversack

over his shoulder; they glared around them for another victim.

Suddenly remembering Terry, I looked fixedly away from the scene of that man's death for a moment or two so that if she followed my gaze she might escape seeing what I had seen. I was wise too late, but when I turned my head, praying that she had not seen, her eyes were tightly closed. She sat with a face like death, frozen in horror. Her hands clutched the heather by her side.

'Terry!' I whispered.

'Is it all over?' she asked in a low voice, without opening her eyes.

'Terry—' I said again. My tongue clave to my mouth. I could not speak except to say 'Terry!' a third time in a rough voice I did not recognize for my own. The smell of cordite drifted up round us. She opened her eyes.

'I think—I think we're safe here,' I muttered. All at once a tumult of shouting and rifle-fire broke out directly beneath us. Venturing to look downhill I saw that two of the fugitives, sole survivors of their band so far as I could distinguish in my hasty scanning of the battlefield, had chosen to climb the shoulder of Meall nan Eacan rather than accompany their friends into the trap of the gully. They were able to cover a certain distance without being seen; I knew the burn they followed; I knew the place where the gorge cut by this burn grew shallow as it crossed the shoulder of the hill. Immediately they reached the shoulder the fugitives were observed. But they had gained a fair start. If they reached the peak of Meall nan Eacan they could keep their enemies at bay indefinitely. Defiles in the precipitous rocks that went up like a giant stairway to the peak made fortresses which two men could defend against a hundred.

As I reasoned thus I recalled our own situation. It seemed desperate at first. We were directly in the fugitives' line of flight. Both hunters and hunted would undoubtedly take us for an enemy; we had to defend ourselves from both sides. It was easy enough for us to ascend to the peak of the hill in safety; but when we came there, what was there before us? My mind pictured the slow descent of the ridge that went down to the bogs round Loch an Doire Uaine. We could, it was true, plunge directly from our height to the valley of the Sluie. That was a trap to be avoided at all costs. Our only hope of safety depended on our keeping to high ground. Once in a valley with the Farrow's steep looming over us we would be cornered at our enemies' leisure.

'They're coming this way,' I told Terry in a thick voice. I peered downhill for the last time to make sure that my reasoning had not led me into needless panic. It was true, I thought, that the obvious course for these two men to follow was straight in our direction. They had surmounted the steepest grade of the hill and they could afford to face a further climb while their antagonists laboured behind them. If these two kept to the ridge on which they had arrived they had a fortress ready made before them. Yet, elated by their success, they might not choose to climb farther, but veering east across the rolling moor, try to escape by speed of foot. I hoped in vain. When I looked back the leading fugitive had gained forty or fifty yards on his companion. He sat down coolly behind a stone to aim deliberately at the rabble below. His rifle spoke once, twice. At the second shot a yelling ruffian flung up his arms; his voice died in the middle of a shout; he tumbled backwards and rolled like a log down the steep. The marksman began to climb again. I led Terry out of our hiding.

We might escape without being seen if the fugitives turned at bay on the crown of the hill. But if they got far in advance of pursuit they might not halt there; instead, chasing in our tracks, they would lead danger after us wherever we went, and if they were swift there was a possibility of their seeing us and overtaking us. I could not hope for much mercy in that event. To men in their plight all other men were dangerous, to be killed before they kill. We were both weak and slow; my side kept dragging; our hunger had weakened us more than we imagined until we came to run. We kept the steadiest pace we could up the shoulder of the hill, down the other ridge towards Loch an Doire Uaine.

Safety awaited us if we got so far as the loch without being seen. From the loch we could slip back into the Little Durc amongst whose caverns there were many dens of refuge that no enemy would dare to assault. If we succeeded in our plan, it would only be by seconds. A dangerous peat-hag divided us from Loch an Doire Uaine.

My thoughts raced ahead of me as we ran. I had never lost my dread of bogs since that time I escaped from the hole in the Durc. I dreaded the traverse of this moss in front of us. Pathless, full of peaty canyons dug by winter floods, it made a labyrinth that I had never attempted to thread in haste until now. I caught Terry's hand to help her along. She clung to me as we scurried downhill.

The noise of firing checked our speed. We ran softly to listen. We heard ragged volleys and amongst them the sound of one rifle at regular spaced intervals.

'They've turned at bay!' I cried joyfully. 'We'll manage now—'

I spoke too soon. Just as we reached the outskirts of the moss a shout from the east, borne loud on the wind, made us pause, and turn. We saw a couple of figures outlined on the ridge of Meall nan Eacan. At first, prompted by hope, I thought it was the fugitives. A burst of rifle-fire beyond the hill-top told me that I hoped in vain. These men we saw on the skyline, who now disappeared as they flung themselves down the steep, belonged to the pursuit. No doubt they were unaware of our existence, no doubt their aim was to circumvent the fugitives and take them from the rear. Nevertheless they had seen us and we were cut off from the Durc, for their viewpoint commanded our entire route. If we dared to enter the Little Durc now we could be trapped like rats. One man posted on each summit that towered over the gorge of the Durc would guard its entire length, its exit and its entrance. Our fastest most happily guided pace across the bog must be slower than the speed with which they came downhill to outflank us.

Our last chance of safety depended wholly on my knowledge of the lie of the ground, of which our enemies

were surely ignorant. I knew that if we allowed ourselves to be
driven away from the stable footing of the Farrow we had only
one retreat, into the wild moss which stretches deep between
Loch Pattock and Strathmashie. On another day than this
we would no doubt have used that dangerous road and saved
ourselves by lightness of foot like moss-troopers. Our feet
were leaden, we were nearing the end of our strength. Unless
we found secure footing soon we must turn at bay like our
fellow-fugitives.

I swung to the right, leaving Loch an Doire Uaine to
the east. The woods by Loch Ericht, which saved me once
before, must be our goal.

We floundered into hags which grew more broken and
treacherous as we advanced. My help was more hindrance
than aid to Terry. There was so much jumping and turning
to be done that while I kept hold of her hand I did but trail
her into bogs which were best gone round. She clung to
me and I dared not try to free myself in case she gave up
heart altogether. Her face was grey, mire covered her from
head to foot, she fell over tussocks and stumbled into slimy
pits. I was in as bad a case. My side was bleeding and my
legs trembled under me when they took my weight after I
jumped. I grew dizzy with staring at the ground before my
feet. When one treads a maze the mind grows dull, bemused
by concentration; to go round an obstacle requires more
strength of will than the weary mind can resolve; taking
each step in dread, we went straight forward over the mire,
descending into peaty canyons to climb their far banks on
our hands and knees, dragging our feet through sloughs
we should have avoided, travelling ever more slowly to the
remote shore.

It was like a nightmare that repeats itself. Even when
we arrived on firm ground we acted as if we were still
floundering in the moss. But in a few yards we reached a
stream and flung ourselves down to drink. The place where
we lay was firm; I have never felt greater comfort than I
had in that instant when I found the stones and turf of the
burn's side under me.

I searched the darkening hills for our enemies, but saw nothing to make us start and run. The wind was shrill. We heard it sounding in the Durc like waves on a shore.

'We should have been there,' I said.

'Where are we going, Hugh?' Terry breathed. 'It's getting dark.'

'A little farther,' I answered. 'Give me your hand, we'll be safe and warm soon.'

'It's cold,' she said. Her teeth chattered violently.

'It's blowing up for snow,' I said. 'Come, Terry, we must reach Loch Ericht before night—just a little longer, honey, and we'll have fire, and food, and shelter.'

THE SNOW IS melting fast; there's still heat in the sun. But it's not a proper thaw. The air is cold behind the sun, and icicles grow in the shadow.

We've felt all the seasons while we lived here. Spring when we came, summer to make us glad, painted autumn—today is winter, time to go before our road is closed. When I shut my eyes I can see winter filling our gorge with drifted snow, the world all blurred with drift.

I forced Terry to leave the cave for a while and breathe fresh air and see the glittering hills; morning painted their snowy summits. Stags were roaring close at hand.

'Did we ever really climb these?' she breathed in awe-struck tones, pointing to mountains whose sides, snow-covered almost to their base, seemed to rise sheer from their dark valleys in steeps that only birds could dare.

'Climb them!' I cried, and laughed. 'Yes, indeed, we ran up and down them like wild goats.'

'They're very steep, aren't they?' she said.

'They seem steeper than they are,' I answered.

I said to myself, 'We did climb them.' Not their apparent steepness made me doubt, but my own faint recollection. The dismal time past was sped. I gazed at the country we traversed a couple of days ago. One of the eagles from the Durc soared into view, climbing in a slow magnificent spiral until it wheeled out of sight, too high over its kingdom for our poor eyes to follow. I thought of its terrible vision of the world, its eyes that saw a realm of hills and a mouse stirring in the grass from that invisible throne in air where now it hid. I thought, where my imagination and my memory faltered, it saw. Our footsteps in the snow amongst the hills were

159

plain to its gaze. Then suddenly I remembered and saw as if with the eagle's sight. I saw the battle in the valley; I perceived our way of retreat to Loch Ericht, and our fire blazing in a cloud of snowflakes, and our return to the top of the Farrow whence we saw other ominous fires gleaming encamped below our cave. Our wanderings were like a map spread out.

'Don't go in,' I begged Terry when she turned to leave me.

'I must,' she said.

'You can't do any good,' I went on. 'You're tiring yourself to death—you haven't rested for more than five minutes together—'

'Soon I can rest,' she said gently. 'It's not his good but my own—making it easier for him has changed me—it won't be long now.'

'Is he weak?' I asked.

'As water. Are you staying here?'

'I'll go in,' I said.

We bent over him. He was nearly done, his breath as feeble as a child's, scarce fretting the silence of the cave. He began to smile and whisper and open his eyes wide. He tried to sit up. Terry put her arm under his shoulders. It was ended before we knew it began; his dead weight lay on her arms. She let him back gently; she stooped to touch his forehead with her lips.

And it's so easy then to die, to die and lose the sun, to open one's eyes and sleep.

'He died quiet,' she whispered. 'He didn't die like a beast, alone.'

No, nor at the crooking of my finger. Christ, how near it was. As I look back the days of our flight assume a dreadful air. Fearful and violent, they belong to destruction. With death eager in our hands we fled from death.

'Terry—' I began hoarsely. She paused from binding his face with a handkerchief and closing his eyes. She laid her hand softly on mine.

'Hugh,' she answered.

'Terry!' I broke out, striving in vain to speak, but

the best I could say was, 'If I hadn't you—if I hadn't you—'

'But you have me and I'm with you,' she murmured. I sank my head on her hands, on the bed where he lay.

'Hush, hush, my child,' she said. 'We've left the past behind us—see! I can smile, look at my face, I've no fear.'

Her face was radiant. I could not escape so soon from thinking of the past. I knew that nothing could ever destroy my knowledge that I alone would never have escaped from the rage of the past. Not like this our sole guest, not gentle and broken like him, but as a wolf, I'd have killed, and died. How can she help me to escape knowing that when every word she speaks convinces me more surely of what I'd be, if she were not with me?

I'll bury him in the valley. *His* eyes are closed. She smoothed his brow and cheeks. Why do we whisper in our cave? He can't hear and death doesn't listen. Death makes his face noble.

I said, 'I thought you were going to die of cold and tiredness. I was mad with fear, Terry.'

'I thought that fire would never burn up,' she confessed. 'We must get ready soon, Hugh. What can we take with us? We can't carry all I'd like to bring.'

She is busy while I write, recalling yesterday, when we came home, and the day before yesterday, when we fled. We came to the wood by Loch Ericht. I had scarcely energy to gather sticks or strength to break them. The branches of the wood were sodden with rain. We made a fire at last. Terry crouched over it, shivering and trembling like one ague-struck. We could not eat for cold. Night encompassed us with dangerous shadow. We jumped when a bird cried or the waves of the loch made a sudden plash.

Our fire smouldered as if never to take, but at length a resinous branch kindled and a blaze flared up. It revealed large flakes of snow drifting slowly on the wind.

'Snow!' Terry cried aghast.

'Snow!' I echoed. 'It might have come more timely,

with all the other days of the year to chose from. What new misfortune must we suffer?' I asked bitterly.

'It might have come more untimely, Hugh,' she answered, 'and showed our footsteps.'

'Or turned these men back out of the hills,' I argued.

'Will it do that?' she asked eagerly. 'And we can go home soon?'

I stared gloomily at the fire. I was without hope. She swayed with weariness as she stooped over the fire.

'Take off your clothes, one thing at a time,' I bade her. 'We can't lie down to sleep in sodden rags.'

I set a long branch across two stones near the fire to make a rack for our garments. We dried them one by one and put them on as they dried. The heat of the fire drove us back into an angle between two rocks where we were sheltered from the rising storm. I hurried out to gather brackens for our couch before the snow hid them and wetted them. The snow came down in huge deliberate flakes. The noise of the wind in the trees grew deeper and we heard the loch beating on its shore, far under us in the thick darkness. When I returned with my arms full of brackens to the light of the fire I was white with snow.

'Is it going to be a bad storm?' Terry inquired anxiously as I shook the flakes from my head and shoulders.

'It's early yet—' I answered dubiously; 'but in this country you never know. We're more than two thousand feet above sea-level here, Terry, anything can happen. It's a wild night. Throw on these roots, lassie, heap up the fire to last until morning. We don't want to waken and find ourselves frozen stiff.' I made an effort to laugh.

'Them all?' she asked. 'Won't the fire be too big—and show us—'

'Anyone abroad to-night will have more thought of shelter than chasing us,' I assured her. 'If we lie here, in the shadow, we can't be seen, however big the blaze. But you couldn't see a town burning through the blanket of this night.'

Our hearts revived with the warmth of the fire. We ate

sparingly; we crept into our pile of bracken and slept soon.
The cold wakened me; I slipped out of our bed to put fuel
on the fire. It had sunk to a heap of grey ashes, but when
I gathered in the butts of sticks which had dropped away
from the centre of the fire they commenced to smoke and
glow in a very short time. I could not tell how much of
the night was past. The world was bright for the snow
had ceased falling and a large moon, nearly full, illumined
the country out of a cold clear sky. I heard Terry stirring
uneasily. She peered from amongst the brackens. Her face
was flushed and confused with sleep.

'Hugh!' she whispered, 'where are you, Hugh?'

'Here,' I replied.

'I slept,' she said.

'Lie still and sleep more,' I bade her.

'I can't sleep more,' she answered. She rose slowly,
stretching her arms. 'Oh, I'm stiff and sore!' she complained. All at once her voice became anxious and afraid.
'Why are you awake?' she demanded breathlessly. 'What
made you waken, Hugh?'

'The cold, Terry,' I said. 'Nothing more.'

'Nothing more? I thought—' She paused as if
revolving what she thought. 'What are we going to do
now?' she went on. 'Can we go home?'

'I don't know,' I began.

'Oh, I'm tired,' she said, and shivered.

'Sleep a while longer,' I said.

'And what are you going to do?' she demanded.

'Oh, I might climb to the top of the Farrow to spy. It's
as bright as day in the open.'

'I'm going with you,' she said.

'But you're tired out!' I expostulated. 'The snow will
be deep in drifts up there—'

She would not be dissuaded. We scattered our fire before
we set out to reach a viewpoint that would command our
cave, its gorge, and the intervening waste. We trudged
mechanically up the hill. Fatigue like poison in our veins
dulled our senses. We were over the round summit of the

Farrow before we halted and saw the cliffs behind our cave
black against the snow in the distance.

'It's a long way off,' Terry whispered.

'Yes,' I agreed, 'and bad going. Can you face it, Terry?'

'What light is that?' she cried. 'See, Hugh! there below
the rocks, near Loch Coulter!'

I stared for a while in the direction she indicated.

'Fires,' I said heavily at length; 'three fires blazing.'

'Fires! but what fires could be there?' she demanded.

'Camp fires,' I returned.

The warmth engendered by our climbing ebbed out of
us. The edged wind went through us as if we were naked.

'We can't stay here on this bare top,' I said. 'The cold will
kill us. Are your feet wet, Terry? Mine are sopping. We'd
best go down—at least we can have a fire there— We
were mad not to take coats,' I said as we descended.

'We never dreamt—' she began.

'We should have dreamt,' I interrupted her roughly. 'We
should know by this time what to expect.'

She kept silent for a time, following me through wreaths
which hid morasses and holes amongst rocks.

'Was it camp fires you said, Hugh?' she asked breathlessly, hurrying to come up beside me. 'Those men are
camped, is that what you meant?'

'Probably for the night,' I assured her with more
conviction than I felt. 'The storm will chase them out
of the mountains pretty soon.'

'I'm glad for the snow,' she said. 'Do you think they're
on their way out of this country?'

'I'm sure of it,' I answered. 'What would keep them in
this bitter desolation?'

'What kept ourselves here?' I asked myself a moment
afterwards, mocking my own hope. We lighted a fire once
again to dry our stockings. It was not yet near day. We ate
the last of our meat. The interminable hours rode over us.
We longed for day to come though we expected nothing from
day but the knowledge that time indeed passed. Before the
sun rose on the peak of the Farrow a string of deer came

up from feeding all night in the wood. I killed a calf with a lucky shot. We wrapped its liver and the best of its ribs in moss and buried them in the embers of our fire to cook. We were ravenously hungry.

'What are we going to do?' Terry asked when we had eaten of that revolting mess of half-cooked meat.

'Do?' I echoed bitterly. 'Wait, nothing but wait.'

'Here where we are?' she went on.

'Oh, not here, nothing so comfortable and easy,' I returned. 'But in the thickest depths of that wood, skulking there—it's time to go.'

We had scarcely penetrated the fringes of the wood when a rustling close by arrested us. Terry, behind me, cried out, 'Hugh! lie down! a man with a gun!'

Upon her words the sound of a shot-gun crashed out and pellets, fired from too great a distance to harm us or else deflected by the branches of trees, pattered round us.

'Lie still!' I shouted to Terry, throwing myself flat. I commenced to worm a way downhill behind a screen of trees in the direction from which the gun fired. Every thought of danger was out of my head. I recked of nothing save lust to avenge on this skulking murderer the misery we endured, the shame and fear of our flight before his like. I heard the noise of feet like a man running, and leapt to my feet in time to see a figure scurrying through a glade, making for the shelter of trees lower down the hill. My rifle came to my shoulder, it steadied, it followed him, aimed full in the centre of his craven back. He was as good as dead. I saw him in imagination tumbling like a stricken deer. Exultation welled up with rage in me; I delayed shooting to savour and protract the sweetness of revenge. My finger crooked on the trigger, taking the first pull, tightening for the second. When I hear my rifle fire I am always surprised, as if in the last instant my hand acted unawares of my head; I waited for that surprise, as rigid as a rock. I had never felt such burning joy as filled me while I waited for my weak finger to crook and drag him down and avenge all we suffered. He bolted for the trees. He was on the edge of the safety he must not reach, though he might grasp it, when Terry's hands seized the rifle. Terry's voice came from the normal world into the dreadful country that I tenanted.

'Hugh! Hugh! Hugh!' she shouted, dragging and pulling the rifle towards her. I stared at her for a second as if she was a stranger, and she at me with eyes alight with terror. Her face worked, her mouth made a soundless shape at words.

'You can't! you can't!' she articulated at last. I let the rifle go and it fell between us in a crevice of rock. I was as weak as if I had come from drowning.

'Terry!' I whispered in horror. I sat down on the ground and hid my face in my hands. It was very silent round us.

I heard her say, 'Hugh—' and a moment later, 'Hugh!' in an urgent voice.

'He's down, he's fallen!' she exclaimed.

I could not bear to meet her eyes. I lifted the rifle and uncocked it. We walked together to the spot where the man lay on his face sprawling with outstretched arms and one leg doubled under him. I gathered his shot-gun from where he flung it when he fled. It was an old hammer-gun so loose in the lock I heard it clank as I caught hold of it.

'He's dead!' Terry cried, starting to run. At her approach the man stirred; he clutched the ground with his hands to drag himself on. When he could not, and his limbs refused to obey, he trembled and hideous whimpering noises came from him.

Terry stooped over him whispering, 'Hush! don't be afraid!'

She laid her hand on his shoulder while she spoke. At her touch he shuddered violently. He uttered such a scream of terror as will never be out of my ears. I hear it now, the voice of incarnate fear to death. What terror had ever we? My heart stood still, my flesh crept. But Terry spoke on, telling him to be at peace. He commenced to sob and rack his throat with coughing mingled with sobs.

'We must lift him,' she said, looking up at me. 'He must be sore hurt.'

When I essayed to move him he screamed again with pain. I raised him in my arms. He had no more weight than a feather. His bare flesh showed through his tattered rags. His face was like a skull, his lips were blue. His blazing eyes closed gently.

'He's dead,' I muttered.

Terry thrust her hand into his breast, through his dirty torn shirt.

'His heart is beating still,' she said. 'What are we going to do with him, Hugh?'

'What can we do?' I asked desperately. 'He's past any help we can give, Terry.'

'Is it so bad?' she whispered. 'What ails him, Hugh?'

'Hunger cold and fear,' I answered grimly.

'We can't leave him here,' she said steadily.

'We can't leave him here,' I echoed. 'But what can we do, where can we take him?'

'Home,' she said.

I looked at her aghast.

'You saw the fires!' I exclaimed.

'Too well.'

'How can we go home?'

'How can we leave this human mortal creature to die? Oh, Hugh, we'd risk our bones to save a dog from agony. What's a little fear, a little danger, compared with his need?'

'Then we'll go home,' I said. 'Are you ready? Can you carry both the rifles?'

He opened his eyes to watch us. We bent over him.

'We're taking you where you'll have fire, and food, and be safe,' Terry assured him. He looked wildly at her.

'Let me go!' he implored. 'Let me go!' He commenced to cry silently. Tears rolled down his grey cheeks from wide panic eyes.

'You must come with us until you are well,' Terry said. 'You can't lie here—you've hurt your leg—'

'Who are you?' he interrupted.

'Friends,' she said.

'Friends!' He laughed in our faces. 'There's no word friends any more.'

He closed his eyes and his head fell to one side.

'We must carry him,' I said; 'he's not fit to walk, even with us helping him.'

'Leave me alone I tell you!' he broke in angrily. A weak delirious rage took him.

'Where's my gun?' he shouted. 'I know what you're after, you want to steal my gun. Give it to me! you can't rob me! let me go! '

'We'll never carry him so far,' Terry said.

'There's no weight in him,' I assured her. 'Now help me up—'

He let himself be lifted without more show of resistance. We set out on our path. I carried him short distances at a time, and rested; when I was not enough revived by my halt we supported him between us with his legs dragging on the ground. I do not think he was ever rightly conscious. We circled the Farrow and Meall nan Eacan by the most level route we could plan. We saw from a long distance off that the fires in our gully were quenched. Our world was empty as of old.

We pieced together the disconnected fragments of his story that he babbled by the way; how he came farther and farther north from the blasted cities hunting for food; how his wife died, and he skulked in hiding every day.

No man was safe, no man had friends, no man helped another, every man's hand was ready to strike.

So we came home to our cave and laid him in our bed and quickened his flickering pulse with a sup of the whisky Duncan brought.

'I'll fetch the haunches of that stag I killed,' I promised. 'To-morrow in the morning early. I know where it lies. We must have proper food, for him too. Rest a while,' I besought Terry. 'I'll make a shake-down on the floor where you can sleep a little, I'll watch—'

'I can't sleep,' she answered. 'Let me sit here, it won't be for long, Hugh.'

I shook my head. 'We came too late,' I said.

'When you bring home the stag, and he's—he's free, what then?' she asked.

'What then? How do you mean "What then"?' I demanded.

'Are we staying here?'

'Where else can we go, Terry? We know the country here. You heard what he said, there's danger every place.'

'I'm not speaking about danger, Hugh.'

'Well,' I asked harshly, 'what are you speaking about?'

'I don't need to answer that for you to know what I mean, do I, Hugh?' she said. 'How safe are we here, if safety's all that counts? Oh, if we run and hide and kill like wolves at bay, we can escape what's come to him, and them in the valley, for a time, for a few weeks—months! —years!—what does it matter how long we enjoy safety like that? Safety to become savages like the men we saw!'

'And if we go do we avoid that?' I cried. 'What use will it serve to run our heads into danger?'

'Great use, if we do it to help other folk, Hugh. We've fed while they starved, we've slept when they wandered distracted with fear.'

'Help other folk!' I laughed. 'Great help we can give! grand helpers we! Assisting others when we can't save ourselves. We've had to go without food too, Terry, and wander distracted with fear. Who'll help us?'

'Ourselves, when we help others. We helped him.' She pointed to the still figure in the hammock.

'Aye, and how were we met? Will others aim as badly as he did?'

'It's a chance we've got to take.'

'Not chance but certainty. Why? To keep the dying flame of life flickering for a few painful extra moments?'

Colour came into her cheeks and her eyes began to sparkle.

'Are you bent on saying things to hurt me?' she cried. 'Should we have left this creature, this fellow mortal, there, alone? You're not quarrelling with me, Hugh, but with yourself, you're saying things you don't believe.'

'Tell me how to say what I believe when I don't know what it is!' I exclaimed. 'Then we should have stayed, we should never have come here.'

'We had to come,' she answered gravely. 'Nothing else would have taught us—this.' Her eyes went to our dying guest.

'Dear, dear lesson!' I muttered.

'All that's worth learning is dearly paid for,' she said.

I went to the mouth of the cave to regard the scene we must forsake. I sat there like a stone for a long time. The stable edifice of our life was collapsing, and like one bewildered by the untimely stroke of chance that wrecks all I could not see a way or light or plan. Our habit of life must alter, to what shape I could not guess. Our stay was ended. Yet as I watched the hills, the shattered custom of our life began to form itself anew. If this hour ended a season of our lives, then it made complete that which it finished; with this regard our life, spent in this place, grew whole and rounded before my eyes.

'We can't carry all our stuff with us,' I said a long time later.

'We must choose what we need most,' Terry said. 'The rest will be safe here; we can come for it if we have use for it.'

If we go from here we'll never come back. I do not speak to tell her what my mind fashions and my thoughts revolve. Why should I vex her with the thoughts that plague my unquiet head? I did not realize she was so much wiser than I, till now. It's best to go, it's wise; but I alone would never go. She'd go; I led her amiss when I brought her here. Or did we behave well when we fled and came here? Have I misled—oh hush, hush, mad head that seeks and seeks for certainty, finding none. It's best to go.

She came to my side.

'We were happy here,' she said.

'Yes,' I answered with an effort to be calm. 'We were happy.'

'Are you sad to leave?' she whispered.

I nodded, I could not speak.

'It's best to go,' I said a moment later.

'Best to go,' she echoed. 'We're human folk, Hugh. Our place is with our fellows. We can't forsake them just to keep ourselves safe.'

I am glad we are going. I see the road we were bound on, that same way trod by the men whose work, smashed relics of living men, lies decaying in the valley. All fated and tied to destruction. Destruction battens on the men who feed it. I lusted for this creature's death. If he died then, not in our hammock, where could I escape? He was as light as a feather in my arms.

Terry burns with pity. Rage and fear live intertwined, to have compassion and lend aid is the only shield that fear will not strike down. I am not afraid. Nothing worse can happen to us than the fate which dogs us every day we quit our cave to hunt for food. Though we meet fate now we face it without dread. We are victors over fate when we choose well, though it destroy us.

IT IS WEARING on to dusk and we are ready to go. We have been hard at work since early morning. Immediately it was light I went for the haunches of the stag I killed on Meall nan Eacan. I could not go yesterday. Terry boiled the venison to carry with us. We have a heavy load to take. Who'd imagine we'd collect so much stuff together into this cave?

Terry is flushed and excited like a girl. We are leaving our diary behind us. Its use is past. I made the last scratch on our wall deep and long to signify an end.

Moments of departure are narrow doors, small portals to the limitless void. We are careless of to-morrow. We know we are going rightly; we carry that safeguard with us wherever we venture. We have been very careful here, planning each day's work in advance, regulating our hours. And happy too.

Terry is bending over my shoulder. She lays her hand on my shoulder.

'I'm ready,' she says.

I shall close the door with a slab of stone. We are happy to go.

TERRY IS DEAD. When I see it there—Terry is dead.
Why do I keep on writing for none to read, rending my heart
to write *Terry is dead*. No, no, this is the pencil she gave me,
nothing's changed, all's the same, this is our cave, our home.
These walls that shelter us—I strike my hands on the rock.
It's rock, this is her pencil, speak to me, Terry. Terry is dead.
She won't speak, she's dead. What's dead, a word, a sound, a
thing of no account? Dead, dead, dead. Waken, blind fool,
din death to crack the frozen air until your ears hear and your
mind knows and your heart believes Terry is dead.

She went dancing before me down into the gully. She never
looked back at the place we were leaving. We climbed the far
side of the ravine, slowly with our load. It was dark when we
came out on the summit.

'Keep close to me,' I said. 'We'll strike the path to
Dalwhinnie soon.'

'I'm here, give me your hand,' she whispered.

We advanced carefully. All of a sudden I heard sounds like
low voices near us.

'Hush,' I said, halting to listen.

She stumbled over a stone and her feet dislodged a loose rock.

A voice cried, 'Who's there?' We stood motionless. The
voice called a second time. Then a rifle fired twice, and once
again. The first two bullets screamed over our heads, the third
struck heavily beside me. Terry seemed to wince, and stumble
against me. She said, 'Hugh!' in a faint voice.

'Don't be frightened,' I whispered. 'We're quite safe.'

She did not answer. How could she answer when she was
dead?

I brought her home. Christ make them stay till morning.

THEY WERE LYING asleep in the same place, four of them together. I watched them while the day lightened. I trained my rifle on them one by one. When it was bright enough for me to see my sights I tried to say, 'Waken!' I could only whisper the word. I said 'Waken!' until my breath obeyed me, and they heard me call. They stirred uneasily, they roused, they sat up. I waited, savouring their fear. I turned the safety catch of my rifle deliberately that they might find me. Their eyes fell on me. They began to go for their rifles. My brain was cold and clear like ice. As I brought them down, one after one, I counted One, Two, Three. The fourth flung himself to one side at the moment I fired. I hit him but not where I aimed. He came to his knees with his rifle in his hands. We fired together. He missed me, but I struck him. I was aiming full at his breast when I saw Terry between myself and him. Her eyes gazed at me, her outstretched hands pleaded. I could not shoot. Her image faded and I jumped to my feet with my handkerchief in my hand. I dropped my rifle as I went towards my enemy. His wavering rifle fired from the hip. I saw it vomit flame before the bullet struck my breast with a force like a hammer blow. In a blur I saw him tumble backwards. I stood alone on the hill-top in the light of the rising sun, staggering like a drunk man, vomiting blood. The deep-ranked peaks climbed out of the morning to circle me round.

I came home, dragging myself along the ground by the failing strength of my arms. I lighted the lamp in our cave. There's very little oil, enough for me. I dragged the slab of stone over the mouth of the cave after me to close our tomb. I can scarcely see. I hear my breath bubbling in my chest.

174

The fire that burned me's quenched. Not long now, Terry. I'll lay myself down on our couch of birch and close my eyes to sleep. We were happy too, Terry. Terry, my love, my heart, my life.

CANONGATE CLASSICS
TITLES IN PRINT